Book Doctor

Also by Esther Cohen

No Charge for Looking

Book Doctor

A Novel

Esther Cohen

COUNTERPOINT
A MEMBER OF THE PERSEUS BOOKS GROUP
NEW YORK

ISBN 1-58243-323-2

05 06 07 / 10 9 8 7 6 5 4 3 2

For everyone who's ever wanted to write a book,
and for the many who've helped me with this one.

Current Project: Finishing Autobiography, *Jews,
Sports, and Weather*
—Bill Scheft, *The Daily News*

I used to think words could do anything. Magic,
sorcery. Even a miracle. But no. Only occasionally.
—Margaret Laurence

Life is God's novel. Let him write it.
—Isaac Bashevis Singer

What Harbinger Singh really wanted was a book. Sometimes, when he was being most honest, he would admit he didn't care very much about the subject. He wanted a book he had written. He didn't know why, and he didn't much care. It could be about bluefish for all it really mattered. Some days though he was more high-minded. He wanted to write a book, or so he'd tell himself, about one critical dimension of life. Love, maybe, or racism, politics or war. On occasion, he imagined all of these unfolding into a great cosmological epic, a very long book, just enough to be considered weighty, with conscious, pyrotechnical prose, characters who talked and sweated elegantly, free spirits who constantly made love with one another inside old red wheel barrows and on moist, green banks of deep lagoons.

Singh himself was a lover of computers. But he made his living in law. Mostly tax law, though he wrote an occasional will. He didn't mind taxes, and although he liked wills less, he didn't dislike them either. He was a hard worker, and could sit in his office for hours on end, engaged in problems replete with cautious details. Taxes, he knew, were a universal problem. He felt that was as close as he could come, in his own way, to truth. As for wills, he told his clients that death told the truth and he was there to help this process along. He enjoyed meetings with clients, enjoyed the chance to ask them personal questions about their lives. And to turn their information into useful statistics.

He was not a handsome man, but he wasn't unhandsome, either. His eyes were large and dark. He was often sparsely bearded, a half circle under his chin, a thin U.

His life was quiet. After a Scotch or two, he would describe it, if only to himself, as unworthy. He felt that destiny had not yet given him his due. His apartment was clean, with reasonable light. He earned sufficient money. He never ran out of toilet paper or soap, and always had enough bottled water. In the living room he'd placed a large rubber plant, green but not overly so, an ugly, quiet plant, never getting in his way. The plant did not make him feel guilty about water. He knew it would survive.

His divorce had not been hard. His wife, Carla, a lawyer like himself though she called herself attorney, had once specialized in pensions. She drifted away from Harbinger around the time he'd conceded his own unhappiness, three years before. Though he loved her still and he didn't quite know why.

They had dinner the first Wednesday of every month, usually steak at a restaurant called Bill's. Their conversations continued unchanged through the years: health benefits, welfare, diet, dogs, the Democratic Party. She often lectured him about public policy reform. In spite of this, he loved her. His wife was a high official, with offices in Albany and New York City. She was not particularly attractive. He liked looking at her, though, particularly her round bare shoulders, and her long, thin, intelligent hands. She'd liked sex well enough in the beginning so that Harbinger, at first anyway, felt reasonably satisfied. They'd drifted rather than broken. After a while, they'd each said they wanted more. He'd meant he wanted more of her. He never knew what she wanted, because she wouldn't say.

He decided he would use his relationship with Carla as the basis for the novel he'd always intended to write. Her name was promising, more promising than her dullish demeanor, her thin brown hair, her elbows so sharp they could hurt, and her breasts that reminded him of two fried eggs without toast. In the novel though, Carla would be transformed into raven-haired Marla. She would be fiery, and consumed. And so too would Harbinger Singh. He decided to call it *Hot and Dusty*. He was the heat and she was the dust. Thinking about this cheered him.

BOOK DOCTOR: For a very reasonable fee, with a guaranteed prompt and gentle reply, I can help you with your book idea. Here are some questions I can answer. Is it good? How strong an idea do you have? Does it work? Is it clear? Does it sing? Is your heart involved? How much? What about characters' names? Are they interesting or believable, like Oblomov, Daedalus, or Captain Queeg? I can help in every category of book, except true crime and romance. I am professional, quick, accurate, and confidential. Arlette Rosen, POB 1000, New York, New York 10036

I

earning a living

Arlette Rosen was the kind of person who earned her living many different ways. Typical of her generation, she fell into life rather than carved it out. A feathery, floating, ageless woman, she had danced in a cage, waited on tables in Spain and Morocco, spent summers in Provincetown and Jerusalem and Ixtapa, taught English, and worked in hotels. She'd had more than one boyfriend with an unpronounceable name. Now she earned her living helping people write their books. She edited those they'd already written, or helped them begin books they felt they wanted to write. Sometimes, they just wanted to visit her on occasion, to talk about books they'd write if they had the time.

This incidental career began with a friend of Arlette's from childhood, a neat woman with small golden earrings, an obvious Alice. Alice had a book at the publishing house where she worked which she didn't have time to edit herself. She asked for help from Arlette, who was then writing articles on nutritious desserts for pets in a magazine called *Rod and Dog*.

"Arlette," Alice said. Her tone was always moderate, considered, fully clear. Unnasal and certain. "You read all the time, I know." Alice, although she worked in publishing, only read manuscripts. "I wonder," and here she paused, holding her phone close to her mouth, as though this was a secret, "if you might help me with a fascinating book. The author is well known. It's a significant subject. Life and Death, more or less. He's a psychiatrist, with a great deal of recognized insight. What he knows about is the human condition. And more. You won't be sorry. This isn't another dull read. That I personally assure you. It's full of the drama of life," she added. "And death, of course. Which is really his one true subject. You'll recognize the name. Harold P. Leventhal. He's always on TV. Even Imus. And he writes. This is his eighth big book. He just needs help."

Arlette was suspicious. Why didn't he write his own book? Was it possible, she wondered, for books not to be written by authors themselves? It seemed odd. Though she could certainly use the money. She liked words, and sentences. She'd edited articles here and there. Alice knew that.

"Fine," she'd said, "let's see," with something like enthusiasm. Alice had the manuscript delivered to her right away. It was called *Life and Death: One Prognosis*. Arlette suggested they try for something more catchy, but Alice said that metaphors made Dr. Leventhal nervous. They were always too imprecise.

Arlette read Leventhal's manuscript very slowly. It was that kind of book, ponderous, sincere, full of parentheticals. It was over a thousand pages of life-and-death examples: what life means, what death means, how the two are linked. He used the passive voice, something Leventhal inexplicably liked. Also the word *inevitable,* which appeared so many times Arlette decided it was his thesis. Life and Death are inevitable. She mentioned this to Alice, who vaguely replied, "That may well be." Arlette never once thought that this reading, this task, could be the start of a career.

They met, Arlette Rosen and Dr. Harold Leventhal, in a serious room for breakfast, in a large French hotel where Leventhal often ate. He always ordered eggs Florentine. Eleven dollars exactly. Leventhal was tall and dour, the kind of man who seemed miserable and entitled. For both of these qualities, and for his unmitigated seriousness, his detailed and ponderous prose, he had received numerous rewards. Arlette tried to match his seriousness. She told no jokes. He asked no questions. She offered no opinions. He spoke at great length, very slowly. He ate very slowly too, getting his money's worth out of his eggs. He explained all his books, those he'd finished, those he'd only begun with an eye to the always tenuous future, his particular versions of *Life and Death*, which he referred to as his principal theme. There were smaller themes for him to plumb as well. He cited, for instance, the relatively important problem of forgiveness. Could it break the cycle of evil? But life and inevitable death were his chosen bailiwick, for now.

She wondered about him, but only a little: He was not the sort of man to inspire much serious consideration. He had no discernible charms, and his physical presence consisted of a very large head, antlike, really, made more so by an overly thin body, fairly long, with a small central bulge above his waist which caused his pants to be far closer to his chest than they might otherwise have been. He wore big, thick glasses that intensified his buggyness, a grasshopper with a PhD. He took them off to make a point, and when he did he blinked continuously.

He was dull, the way people are who study singular subjects for entire lifetimes. They met in early July, and that summer Arlette lived with Harold P. Leventhal's book. The P was for Prescott. She read the book, early mornings, and late at night. She felt his long sentences, his moreovers and thuses become an ongoing part of her life. Some days she resented it, resented his deliberate ponderousness, his stuffiness and his lack of grace. Some days she was hot, and took the train to the beach, forgetting him altogether.

She began to realize she liked this work, liked the freedom of someone else's sentences, liked being able to change, in intuitive ways she just knew, small details here and there. And although Leventhal often fought her, generally preferring his own words to hers, she sometimes won, presenting herself as an expert. He believed in expertise, so he didn't question hers all that much.

She knew she was not an expert in anything more serious than where to buy the best pistachio nuts, or where to find a good Yemenite restaurant in Brooklyn. So it surprised and even pleased her a little that she was comfortable enough with Leventhal's *Life and Death*, with trying to find an order that would add up to a book, with revising, culling, editing, moving parts around. In the end, she'd made it clearer, shorter, a little bit better. When the first review appeared, a long, scholarly, pompous review by an English expert on this very same subject, a review full of admiration, even praise, Arlette felt a small yet perceptible glimmer of satisfaction. So when Alice called again, pleased with her work, to ask Arlette to work on a book she deemed even more important, a book about rhesus monkeys, Arlette, without a second thought, said yes. In a year, she'd become a full-fledged book doctor. She even received many queries in the mail. A few each day.

June 13

Dear Arlette Rosen,

Can you help me?

I'd like to write a book called *Coping With Disappointment: What to Do After You've Finally Found Your True Inner Self.* I'm sure there's a huge market. The self-help audience for this message is infinite.

I am an alternative and inner self professional. My areas of knowledge include Aromatherapy, Bach Flower Remedies, Polarity, Reiki, Alexander Technique, Shiatsu, Reflexology, Homeopathy, Psychic Healing, Feng Shui and Acupuncture.

I need help in the formulation stage. Marge Schaefer, a client of yours (*I Can Do Anything* and *So In Fact Can You*) gave me your address.

Yours in hope,

Star Dawn Planet

a/d/b/a/ Olive S. Cooper

To: Arlette Rosen

Jack Vance at Princeton gave me your name. He said you'd remember. Whatever that might mean.

I'd like to send you *Black Box,* my 32 candid interviews with men and women in the phone sex business. These interviews were conducted by myself. (I am Claeyton Howard, author of *Saul*

Bellow: A Long, Productive Life, and *Philip Roth: Visionary, Misogynist, or Both?). Black Box* is a high concept, really. (By the way, if you think *White Box* might be better, or even just *Box,* I am relatively open.) One that works.

Black Box is the first book which has a sealed pull-out section (the book will have a male and female edition, red and blue. Also, perhaps, straight, and gay) which can actually bring the reader to orgasm. Guaranteed. I can't imagine anyone from 12 to 92 who wouldn't want a copy. It might not become a classic, but the novelty should put it into the *Waldo* category. Don't you agree?

Jack Vance suggested your usefulness to me because I am more or less a concept person. The details are how you might be of service. (Who was it who said God was in the details? I believe a famous painter. Perhaps Rubens.)

I've got the interviews, and can have them transcribed. But the editing, the order, and that kind of thing I'd like you to do. I'll pay you, of course. Reasonably well. Are you interested, or at least, somewhat curious? Do say yes.

Claey

HELLO OUT THERE IN ELUSIVE UNKNOWN SPACE.

I have written a deconstructivist novel, called *Gone,* or *Minus.* The subtitle will be *Quattrocento Beauty.* Others have tried. Roland Barthes for one. But you can't really read him. Mine you can read. It's as accessible as the shattered (missing) object in cubism, and the atonality of music. It's a charming, shabby, intimate, accessible, sexual, disconcerting novel about freedom. There are six characters, and they're all gone by the end. Just gone. (Not dead.) All that's left is an omniscient frog. It's not like Beckett, or Pirandello either. Mine are not searching (although they are of course alienated). Also, all six are female, from 18 to 88.

(Where they go doesn't matter so much as that they leave. It's a book about leaving, in fact.)

I need some help. There are times the idea becomes too looming. I feel that instinctively. If you could highlight those areas in yellow for me, I would be grateful.

I can pay. I got a grant.

Are you free?

(Not ultimately, but to do this job?)

Fisher Smythe, PhD

2

olives

Arlette had worked on sixty-four books by the time Harbinger found her. She'd chosen those books out of hundreds of queries, maybe more. She placed ads in writer's journals, on bulletin boards, and in bookstores, but most of the mail came from strangers who had gotten her name from clients and friends. She found out very quickly that the world was full of unwritten books, ideas, and intentions. Many people, old, young, educated or not, poor, rich, in-between, wanted a book that was theirs.

Almost every day, she received letters about books. These letters were her life. They were her friends and her children. They were her secret mantra, her addiction, her way of living. They were funny and sad and alive, and she waited for them, often saving them to open at very particular moments: at three o'clock on a winter Wednesday when nothing else could possibly happen, or at six on Thursday nights in the spring. They were rituals, small holidays. She carried them with her on trips and when she went visiting. Parceling them out each day like vitamins. She saved each query in a file, for no particular reason except that she liked getting so many letters from strangers. She didn't want to let them go. And she answered them all, trying to say something more than No.

She often chose which manuscripts to take by how the packages felt. If she could feel something inside the envelope, some sign of life, if the handwriting had a portent to it, if a certain heft was there, or a lightness, or if she just liked the way the envelope looked—the placement of stamps, the color ink, the texture of the paper—she'd take it on.

She had some rules. No violent books. No books where the author used flags or love stamps on their query letters. No books that were racist or sexist or stupid. No books with *light* in the title, or *dolphin, dog,* or *whale.* No books that made fun of Jewish mothers. No survivor stories. No books about rocks, or money, or rockets, or rivers, or snow. No books with characters named Pops, or Peeps, Mary Lou, Anne Marie, Jean Marie, or Jean. No books with titles in Latin. No books with the word *sweet* anywhere in the text. Or *testosterone* or *self-love.* No books that she could forget too quickly.

Harbinger came to her through a friend of a friend. She could tell, by the overly polite professional way he called her Miss Rosen, that he was trying hard, but she knew too that his book was probably not very good. In the beginning this feeling about authors bothered her. She knew good books were rare, although everyone who came to her more or less believed that theirs, the story they chose to tell, would be the way they would at last receive their due. The rest would logically follow: recognition at long last, and grants, good jobs, rewards, and then, Eternity.

At first what amazed her were the stories, their range and subject matter, the countless ideas people had for their books. Some wrote novel after unpublished novel. Others had an idea, and just knew it should be a book. Some loved Asian history, or Einstein, or making chairs, or egg recipes, or researching revolutions, or why some people sneezed and others didn't, how people prayed, what wellness meant. They wrote often, no matter what their lives were like, no matter what got in the way.

Arlette was a person full of doubt. She doubted she could do very much except fix a sentence, replace one word with another: *celadon* for *light green, ecstasy* for *intense happiness.* Even her changes, her reordered paragraphs, were never absolute. She knew they could always be better. So could her life. She imagined herself otherwise, a person she would never be, confident, sure. Unambivalently idealistic, committed to large goals, alongside elegant, memorable sentences. She wanted, if she was entirely honest, to sit in a room—it didn't matter where—and write: every story she knew, every story she didn't know. She wanted to describe earthy strangers, married lovers, Jerusalem, Jackson Heights, white peaches, home-care workers, the hands of young children. She hardly wrote at all.

But it was always somehow there, right below the surface. She imagined it would begin with the weather: a Turgenev storm maybe, wet but not too cold. Jerusalem dampness, melting to light pinkish sun. Dampness that held the smell of kerosene. Sun would hover behind clouds, perceptible but barely. She pictured characters having a picnic under an ancient tree, twisted and beautiful, an eternal tree along a rill.

The muezzin would climb up onto his tower, and his sounds would cover the picnic, adding eternal song.

She could smell light dust, and greenness. Her characters would eat bright red luscious tomatoes, milky white sheep's cheese, and shiny olives wet with garlic and fragrant oils. They would carry their bread in colorful handkerchiefs. Sometimes, she imagined her characters fighting. She did not ever actually begin in earnest although she often took notes, and wrote ideas, and names in particular, along the margins of magazines, on envelopes and bills, which she would then save in a file marked "Jerusalem, One Day."

She always took notes on trips. She would jot down names of small-town beauty shops, Hair-em Salon, or Hair Today, or of strangers she'd meet on buses, Middle Easterners in particular, Jiryis Jiryis, Vartanoush Guroyian, Aryeh Moore, thinking someday she'd weave them together into a coherent, melodic narrative wail, set on top of Jerusalem's hills, replete with Hasidic bike boys and Hadassah ladies gone wild, Arab olive wood sellers and Palestinian philosophy PhDs, German doctors and thin Swedish tourists. Jerusalem seemed like the only real place for her novel. Not for its holiness, though holiness never hurt. But because of its crazy contradictory powers, its deep memorable fragrance, and its ancient white stones. And the unlikely lovers so possible there, Coptic clerics and Danish dancers, white-garbed nuns and Swedish men, young handsome rabbis, long Dutch girls, dark Palestinians in complex ménages. It was, for her, a place of beauty, of pain, of humor and presence.

Unlike Venice, achingly beautiful but wetly remote, or Bali, captivating but full of frightening frogs and monkeys, Jerusalem seemed full of stories she knew in her blood.

She also knew too well how easy it was to fail. She had seen, over and over again, how readily one could write an empty sentence, create characters who barely mumbled, tell a story no one wanted to hear. To write a book that was not Shakespeare or Joyce, was not rhythmic or engaging, was not gentle or angry or even honest. These things scared her.

Still books obsessed her, obsessed her for what they could be. She'd been a book addict all her life, always reading. She was a difficult reader, and knew that it was easier to criticize people who were trying than to actually write herself. Like a single aunt, other people and their books became her life. She would meditate on occasion, go to movies, see friends for dinner, but it was books that took over her days, all those characters, all those plots and theories and stories about everything from Elvis's hairdresser's memoirs to the *Exxon Valdez*. These stories became her life.

Along with Jake.

Jake was very opinionated. Sometimes she joked that his thinness was the result of his feeling that no food was good enough to enter his body. Jake, when people asked what he did, would reply that he was In Film. He meant that he worked in a place called Film Focus, a nearly Italian downtown theater, small and modern, dark and imposing, that saw the world as a series of film festivals organized largely by subject. All you could eat at the Focus was espresso with biscotti, almond or chocolate. White sugar was taboo.

Jake ran a series called Point of View. As he explained to Arlette many times, not everything was a point of view. His point of view specialty was drama.

Nature was the example he'd give. A documentary that you'd see on PBS on black bears in Montana was definitely not a point of view. Much else was, however, and many evenings, Arlette would watch the point of view Jake had chosen. In a way, their work was similar, though Jake did not agree. He believed that film transcended written language. That it was more, and better, that moving image was comparable to nothing else. That it was as close as you could come to the dream life really was.

Jake saw film as a real chance for audience. For very large numbers. Particularly because of videos and DVDs. Of course, Jake's own tastes had nothing to do with audience. He liked experimental Czech films, sometimes animated, films that only showed at midnight during the week at the Focus. Films about puppets, and music, and death. He liked film noir, and had many favorite directors: Kurosawa, Scorsese, Coppola, Herzog, Bertolucci.

They argued about this often. They'd met at a Fellini retrospective at the Focus, three years before. Arlette had just broken up with a Palestinian revolutionary named Fuad. She felt relieved. Fuad always made her feel guilty, as though injustice was chiefly her fault.

Jake had recently ended a ten-year relationship with a Frenchwoman named Emilie. Emilie was also In Film. She wrote scripts, which Jake sometimes called post-Godardian. Emilie made a film once too, a film that Jake admired. She called it *Breath*. Jake had three copies. He referred to her film as a discourse.

Arlette knew he took his terms very seriously. In fact, Jake took everything seriously, more or less. He only wore black clothes. His hair was carefully short. He smoked black Gauloises, and whenever he wasn't watching a movie, he was reading a book about movies. What was funny was that Arlette loved him. It was not a very rational love. It was just there between them, unwieldy and difficult and, occasionally, painfully sweet.

Sometimes though she felt love was not for her. She could read about it, and often did. She listened for hours to the details of friends' lovers. But she rarely talked to anyone about herself and Jake. She'd had many lovers, and a few had been large and overwhelming, messy and difficult and so consuming it was hard to do much else. Those relationships had taken over all her life. They'd been almost like religion. And that's not what she wanted.

With Jake, her life was intact. Jake had his own apartment. They each liked that. Neither one of them had to compromise. Arlette liked white towels. Jake liked black. Arlette liked mornings. Jake stayed up all night. On the nights they spent together, they took turns at where to sleep. They were together, but not so much that it got in anyone's way. They were both 35. Each of them felt they knew, although admitting this was another matter, that their lives were more or less fixed. Arlette, for all her ideas and her notes, knew she'd probably never write her novel. She found this sentence impossible to say, so never did, even to Jake.

Jake often talked about his movie. He'd been writing a screenplay for years, and although he never gave it to her to read, Arlette knew he had something there, something more than beauty-parlor names and vague ideas about Jerusalem and love. This could have been why they stayed together, why their relationship persisted. Arlette, although she said often that she would like to travel again, something she'd done for years, knew how much she wanted to stay in one place. To sit still. To plant a flower garden, to raise a dog, to slowly read books of poems. To join a peace group, Fellowship of Reconciliation or Amnesty or Friends, and write letters to prisoners. To sit still and watch, after years of whirling around.

Her life, or so she imagined, was very different once. Then, she saw the world as possible, as interesting and large, a full, round circle, water and sunsets and warm, open people eating Greek meals and singing. She had wandered from place to place, working odd jobs and falling in love, all for what seemed like minutes at a time, only minutes. Now though, for reasons that weren't all that easy to describe, she felt like a small dot in a very large blackness, babbling on. She couldn't pinpoint this change, or the moment when things started to look different. She knew though that her days seemed incomplete, and she knew too that this feeling was not about to change. She could easily turn into one of those people she disdained. Someone had sent her a book proposal about this once, called *The If Only Syndrome*. If Only there was money, or time, or a place to work. She hadn't worked on the book, but she'd sent a note back. If Only I Could, Then I Would. The author had replied to her rejection. This had happened only once before. But You Can, he'd said.

Ms. Rosen,

I have a high-concept idea that I'm sure is worth
money, and what I need is some help fleshing it
out. I'm sure you won't need more explanation than
the title: *Firm: A Lawyer's Exercise Guide*. A
lawyer myself, I know how much we sit. No other
choice is available to us. And I know first hand
how dangerous the consequences are, from the
perspective of flesh. Even in court, it's rare that
we are actually standing. And there especially, we
can't move around very much. I propose developing
a series of exercises created especially for
lawyers. If this idea is as successful as I would
imagine, then we can continue with specialized
guides for virtually every profession. Lawyers buy
books. I know that for a fact. And I can easily

imagine *FIRM* on every shelf. Would you like to participate in this project, as a partner?

Yours,

John Thurow

Dear John Thurow,

What a commercial idea. I wish I could help you. I don't know much about exercise, or law. I ought to though. Maybe your books will help me when they're published. All Best

AR

3

meetings

Harbinger Singh met Arlette Rosen at three o'clock on a Wednesday afternoon. It was early July, too warm for his dark brown wool suit, but he liked the suit, liked the fact that the color nearly matched his skin. He liked it enough to wear as often as he could. He thought of himself as brownish, but in fact, he was more a deep golden yellow, the yellow of Indian sun. He called it full sun himself, preferring it to full moon. He thought of himself as powered by sun, though profoundly influenced by the moon. Usually, he thought very little about color, his or other peoples. It wasn't the kind of detail that occupied Harbinger Singh.

He was a man of methods and goals. He made lists, then crossed out the tasks he'd accomplished. He would move undone jobs from one list to another, and sooner or later, the neat equidistant lines indicating completion would cover all his pages. Harbinger saved these pages in a desk in a drawer, numbered by date, and although the entries were barely discernible, and he couldn't quite remember just what he had done, still the several hundred pages he kept in three black folders gave him deep satisfaction.

On occasion he had an affair, but they never amounted to much. He told himself that these affairs, though even the word was too big, these quick forays into sex, maybe, were a natural part of his marriage to Carla, who wasn't very interested in sex. While they were still married, he became lightly involved, only twice, with women he'd met through work. Though he'd never thought, even for a minute, that either relationship was love. He loved Carla absolutely. She had work to do, and her work, which put them both into a top tax bracket, took priority over everything else, even pleasure. On occasion, she had something that could possibly be described as an urge, but her urges were not memorable, and her thoughts barely wavered from her job, even then. After sex, she'd often bring up office problems, seeking Harbinger's advice.

After he and Carla got divorced, he took a few women to dinner, but he found, on those slow and painful evenings, that they had less to say to one another than he and Carla had. Though his relationship with Carla had been more or less flat, and he didn't know why he should love her, still he did. This love burned through him. He was always there. He thought about Carla day and night, although there was no reason to be so obsessed with a woman so careful, so clean. So rational. She even wore pajamas.

On their last night together, before she moved out, into a big clean building with a doorman and a gigantic parking lot, they had what turned out to be the first of their weekly dinners.

Harbinger asked why she supposed they'd married. Carla, who often spoke as though she were addressing her senior high school class with her valedictory speech, something she had done nearly twenty years before, on the subject of social policy and moral responsibility, replied in a softer tone. "No one knows why they marry. If they say they do, they're pretending. I suppose we married because we respected one another and our work is somewhat compatible. We were not unhappy," she added, which was, for Carla, a gentle remark. She would not say more.

"I suppose you're right," Harbinger replied. "But what about," and here he paused, wondering whether the word was appropriate for this particular occasion. Then he just went ahead. "What about love?" he asked. "What about love?" Carla did not seem thrown, or even upset. "A major subject," she replied. "We don't know much about it, I guess. No one does. Certainly not us." She smiled vaguely.

Harbinger imagined he would write this scene very differently. He imagined Carla crying, desperate to be together again. Not cool, but rather enraged. On the edge of her seat with anxiousness. Silently and not so silently pleading Please Take Me Back Harbinger Singh.

"But you loved me once," he said sadly, as though it were a question. "Of course," she replied. "Of course I did."

"Then what changed?" Harbinger asked. He did not want to sound mournful or pitiable, only interested. "What changed between us? And if it's all the same, why did we both agree so easily to divorce?"

"Nothing's changed," she said, and then she added very familiarly, "Harbinger." She rarely used his name.

"I see," he said, and then decided that he would rewrite this altogether. They'd both be crying, unable to eat, and they would decide that parting would be a horrible mistake. Then they'd return to their old apartment, warm, dark, full of rugs and Indian music, and make love in a way that surprised them both. Maybe the book should end there.

Harbinger thought of this as he rang Arlette's buzzer. He wanted the word *wild* in the title. He read somewhere that it was one of those words, like *dogs* and *whales,* that people always liked. *Wild End,* he thought. *Wild Whale, Wild Dog,* or even *Wild Taxes.* Taxes were something he knew well. Even so, he felt wedded to *Hot and Dusty.* He would ask Arlette Rosen her opinion.

Arlette had dressed for Harbinger Singh. She tried to look officially artistic for her writers, knowing and literary, reasonably in charge, and sure enough of what she was doing. Aspiring writers, she knew, concentrated on these details. She imagined herself a book doctor, and so she often wore white, even in winter. For Harbinger Singh, a lawyer with literary ambitions, Arlette wore a white cotton skirt, plain, nearly Victorian, and a French cotton T-shirt, very simple. She was tall and thinnish, and her face, in the right light, had a handsome cast, like a Russian feminist explorer on a silver coin. But she could look impenetrable too, the kind of woman who'd be too hard to please. She wore earrings, thin silver snakes from Bali that decorated her ears. On her wrist was a silver bracelet, old and foreign looking, surprisingly soft. It moved across her wrist in a light and girlish dance.

Harbinger looked at her and thought to himself, Not Too Bad. Arlette looked at Harbinger and wondered about his suit. She tried not to be as judgmental as she was, but this was an effort.

"Do come in," she said, and he extended his hand first, to shake.

"Harbinger Singh," he said unnecessarily, and pumped her hand up and down for a minute. His hand was straightforward and strong.

"Well, hello," he said again, when she didn't seem to respond right away.

"Please come in," she said. "Right in here, if you don't mind. I only have two rooms. I've thought about renting an office for years." Here her voice trailed off, as though reasons why not were not of their concern right now. "But this is enough," she added.

He did not look around her living room. He just sat down. The couch was a faded velvet, a pinkish that once might have been more red. The cushions were small satin squares with pieces of embroidery she'd gathered on her trips. She'd sewn them on herself. He did not look at them. She could tell right away that he didn't care much about visual details. Usually, writers who came just began to talk and Harbinger was no different. Arlette sat across from him in an old rocking chair. She leaned forward with her spiral notebook and a pen.

"I've always had the intention of writing," he said. "A book primarily, although there are other possibilities when that is finished. A play is in my head," he said. "I call it *Queens,* referring to one of my homelands. A biography of Gandhi." Then he added. "And the poems."

"What about them?"

"There are the poems," he said, shyly. "I haven't written them yet. But of course, I am a poet. Aren't we all? It's in our souls, I believe."

"I see," said Arlette. "And where would you like to begin?"

"With the novel," he replied. "I just need a little help. A push in the right direction, because I know it is right in my head. The story is there in front of me. I just need time to put it down. And a little help with the process. I am sure." Here he smiled at her, and crossed his legs, swinging his right foot nervously back and forth arhythmically. Arlette tried not to stare at his moving leg.

"What will your book be about?"

"Well," he replied, leaning into the cushions on her couch as though he were preparing to tell a very long story. "Well," he said again. Then he looked at her earnestly, as though she were a client of his, someone with a minor but troubling problem with her taxes. Underpayment, perhaps. Or avoidance for three years. Without the personal resources to rectify her problem right away. Coming to him for advice.

"Well," he said a third time. "Here I go. I've been thinking that I would like to call the book *Wild*. *Wild Taxes,* possibly. Although *Hot and Dusty* has always been in my mind. A year or so ago, when I started conceiving this novel, it was very different. Then I called it *At the Bench,* or *Up to the Bench*. Or even just *Bench*. At first, it was a courtroom novel, which all took place in a small dark room, very formal, presided over by a woman judge from Calcutta," he said, and smiled. But he paused for a minute, almost lost. Unexpectedly nervous. He recovered quickly, though, and continued. "She had her training in England. Very smart. You can't put one over on her. Her name, for your information, is May. Un-Indian, that. But we have had many influences. The first book, not actually the first, but last year's book, we'll call it for clarity's sake, was about a murder. A man murdered his wife because she made his life impossible. After her death he found a master plan in her top stocking drawer in the closet. It was to murder him. She had enlisted the support of his mistress, who'd secretly become his wife's lover. I know this plot is not a first. But I intended to make it different through my choice of particulars."

Arlette nodded.

Harbinger suddenly seemed very confident. He looked Arlette in the eye, and spoke a little too loudly.

"Now, though, something else has replaced this idea. Now I would like to try something we can call for today just *Wild Taxes*. Not a murder. A simple love story, of a passionate love that failed. Circumstances wouldn't allow it to be," he added, and looked satisfied with his own explanation, as though he'd finally said something he'd wanted to say for years.

"What were those circumstances?" Arlette asked, and wrote the word *circumstances* under Harbinger's name. Her authors' files were only words, jotted here and there.

"If I were to say now, I might lose the impetus to begin," said Harbinger Singh. "I don't know that I am able to tell you just like that. There are only two characters, however. Their relationship is set against corruption all around. Incest, murder, death, homelessness, war, the world," he said vaguely. "Big corporations, the British, others whose motives are less than admirable. You know," he added, and she nodded. "A difficult world," he said. Moslems, Christians, Hindus, Jews." His voice trailed off.

"Yes," said Arlette. "Very difficult."

"One of the reasons why I have in mind to write a novel," he continued, "is that the tax business, while it is lucrative enough, is not very satisfying on a spiritual level. I'm sure you understand this."

"Yes," said Arlette. She was trying to keep an open mind. She knew all writers were nervous, particularly in the beginning. Still she felt a twinge of contempt for Harbinger Singh. And taxes. There was something about choosing to do taxes that bothered her.

"I enjoy my work," he said, as though he knew what she was thinking. "It gives me a chance to see many people. To ask them questions, and hear about their lives. To help them," he said, then added, "even somewhat. I have no illusions on that score." He looked at her and smiled, as though she were the client, not him.

She liked him a little better.

"And you?" inquired Harbinger. "And you?" he repeated. "When I meet new people, I often explain myself, to put them at ease. Perhaps we can do the same. Let's begin with your process, and your fees. I am interested in both. I can describe more of my character if that will help you. I collect takeout menus. One of my few idiosyncrasies. I enjoy them. They are peculiar artifacts of Americana. In fact, if I were an archaeologist, they would be my typology. They are numbers and words in lines, so they fulfill other needs of mine as well."

"Well," she said, not knowing what to say about his menus. "My fees, first of all, are yours. I receive what you get per hour. In your case, I assume that's about one hundred dollars, more or less. But you'll have to tell me."

He looked annoyed. "But you have no overhead," he said. "No secretarial help, for example. No equipment. No expenses except for your pen," and here he smiled. "I don't even see a fax machine. Not that you need it of course. I am making no judgments, I can assure you of that. I myself am a technical caveman. Or is it cave person? Do forgive me."

"I am providing a service that is hard to evaluate financially," she said. "I'm sure people have this problem all the time with their taxes. What is a novel worth? One dollar? One million dollars? Somewhere in between? What is it worth for you to write your novel? Fifty dollars? Three thousand? I'm afraid the way I resolve this question for myself and for my clients is to suggest that my work is equivalent in value to theirs." Arlette stood up, moving around the room like a teacher in a classroom. She felt unsettled, and yet she'd said these same words many times. "I don't think, of course, that money and art are connected. A wonderful poem, for instance, is worth millions. But a bad poem's not worth nothing. I want to make it possible for everyone to work in this way if they want. If you don't find the process acceptable, of course I understand. Perhaps you can find someone cheaper," she added. "As for how I work, that depends completely on you. I give you exercises to help you think about your characters. To make them real. But you're the one who tells the story. I help you do that," she added. "When we're through, you'll have written enough to make you comfortable with the process," she said. "You'll have a better idea what you're doing once you start."

"I'd like some time to consider this," he said. "The finances add another dimension to the equation. I thought it would be cheaper. Not that I am disparaging your services. Not at all. But I will think carefully, and call you in a few days. In any case, I will be happy to pay you for this initial consultation," he said. "Please," he smiled, and stood up, removing his wallet tentatively. It was old brown leather, well used. He opened it toward her, to display very neat bills, a large enough stack. She imagined them organized by serial number.

"No," she said. "Our first meeting is free. Everyone is entitled to one free session in all service industries. Don't you agree?"

"Not entirely," he said. "That might put many out of business. Just one question, by the way. Will I be able to make enough from the sale of my novel to cover your expenses?" His question seemed innocent.

"This is about writing," she said. "Only writing. But you're not the first one to ask me that question. There's a poet

I like very much, named Edward Field, who wrote a poem called "Writing for Money." I learned it years ago. It goes like this:

> My friend and I have decided to write for money,
> he stories, I poems.
> We are going to sell them to magazines
> and when the cash rolls in
> he will choose clothes for me that make me stylish
> and buy himself a tooth where one fell out.
> Perhaps we will travel, to Tahiti maybe.
> Anyway we'll get an apartment with an inside toilet
> and give up our typing jobs.
> That's why I'm writing this poem,
> to sell for money.

"I can give you a copy, if you like," she said.

"Oh no, that won't be necessary," he said. "Perhaps later on I may have the need for a copy. But not right now. Please don't stand," he said. "I am capable of going without undue fanfare. But thank you," he said. "I feel optimistic."

Then he left. She wasn't sure if she'd hear from him again. She waited a few minutes, until he was clearly gone, to pick up her mail from downstairs. She thought about him, but very, very briefly. A small moment.

There was only one letter, in a brown recycled envelope. She often wondered if recycled envelopes had been envelopes before. The handwriting was cheerful, circular, a little too young.

Hi Arlette,

I don't know if you remember me, but I remember you! We were on the same dorm floor. Different ends

of the hall. I had brown hair and was very
slightly overweight. My room was 315.

I got your address (obviously) from Susan Davis.
She told me you're a book doctor. What an unusual
job. I'm sure you meet a lot of fascinating people.

By now, you're probably wondering why I'm writing.
Well you'll never believe this. I was a sociology
major, so I'll bet this seems unlikely, but I
wrote a novel. It's based on a true story. I don't
feel I can do it justice with a plot summary.
(Remember those from book report days? I read in
my How to Query Handbook that people still want
them. Can you believe it?) But maybe helping with
plot summaries is one of the things you do. The
working title is *Go Figure,* and it's the story of
my life. (It sounds like it could be a book about
keeping track of your money I guess. But it
isn't.) Speaking of money, I really don't have any
idea what a book doctor costs. Do you charge like
a medical specialist? My ex was an ENT doctor. Can
you give me an estimate? Or do you have to see the
patient first. Ha Ha. Should I just send it to you?

Yours for the lavender and white!

Debbie Altman

Harbinger Singh quickly replaced Debbie Altman in
Arlette's mind. Though she wasn't sure why.

4

polka dots

Arlette and Jake had plans to see a performance artist named Night Shade do his monologue downtown. They'd intended to meet for dinner first, at one of the few restaurants that Jake liked, called Double Spring Roll on Spring Street and West Broadway. Arlette, for reasons she couldn't name, felt angry at Jake as she waited for him. When he arrived, handsome and distant, smiling at her in his familiar way, she responded a little too loudly. "It's much too trendy in here. It's too art-directed." She spoke as though he were to blame.

"You sound like Mia Farrow in that bad Woody Allen movie," he said. "where she falls in love with Joe Mantegna and turns into Mother Teresa." He smiled at her. "You're the one who always says that righteousness is dangerous."

"I've been in an odd mood all day," she said. "I keep repeating 'Life Is a River, Life Is a River,' as a way to relax, but it just sounds like a book title."

"I hope you haven't been working on some self-help book," Jake replied. "You know, I've always thought self-help was a Christian idea. Jews don't have the notion that they can be redeemed. We try to understand what we can, we make attempts, like Freud did, or Marx, or all the Talmudic scholars. We study, instead of repent." He looked pleased with himself.

"You think in such superior male terms," she replied. "And you know how I feel about the whole 'chosen' syndrome. It's awful."

"What's with you? Did something happen?"

"Nothing," she said. "Truly nothing."

"I thought a new writer was meeting you to talk. You always like that."

"He did, and I do."

"Who was it?" Jake asked. "Maybe that's the problem here. Maybe you're mad at him."

"A tax lawyer. That's all. And he's writing a book, or says he wants to. They all say that. He doesn't seem to know what it's about."

"So far, so good," said Jake. "You like people who want to write books. I thought you believed it was all about the effort. The process. That people who don't try are the problem."

"I don't try, and he does." She looked straight at Jake, and could feel herself start to cry. "I judge instead," she said. "And find myself lacking."

"Looking at what in particular?"

"All of it," said Arlette. "Start to finish. A to Z."

"If this is about Night Shade, just tell me," said Jake. "Because we don't have to go. We can stay here all night. Night Shade is just an interest of mine. Besides, he's performing through Thursday. We could go somewhere else. Or just go home," he added. He looked around the restaurant at the large black-and-white blowups of noodles on the wall, and suddenly understood she wanted to leave.

"We have no home," Arlette said, more resigned than angry now. "We have chosen not to make one, out of some idea of mutual convenience. Neither one of us wants to compromise. What would happen, for instance, if you used a white towel? Or lived in a space with unbearable chairs? Stuffed, for example. Semivintage."

Jake looked stunned. He leaned across the table to grab Arlette's hand, but she wouldn't let him. His face, usually handsome and clear, a strong face, looked frightened. "Did this tax guy say something particularly upsetting?"

"No," she exhaled. "Only that he wanted to write a book. It wasn't what he said. It was who he was."

"Well you've heard what he said a thousand times. Maybe more. Has it ever bothered you before?"

"No," she said. "I will help him. It's not that. I don't know what it is."

"Do you want to go to graduate school? Maybe we should take a vacation. I'm tired myself," said Jake. "We can go to Maine. Or is that too Waspy? Montana's supposed to be beautiful. We've never been west. How about the Caribbean? We can get a cheap flight to Jamaica. And then there's Costa Rica. So many people have said it's paradise."

Jake was not usually so concerned with her moods.

"I'm not so happy myself. I've lost my point of view," he said, "which is ironic, given that it's the name of my series."

"I wonder if I ever had one. I've become a nature documentary, without the beautiful scenes of pollinating bees."

"Well, at least it's not your job, anyway."

"That's where you're wrong," she said, and reached out for his hand. She felt endlessly conflicted about herself and Jake. Her moods often shifted wildly.

"Does this mean we can actually eat? All I've had today is a thousand cups of coffee."

"Yes," she said, "but I don't think I can stand Night Shade. Not tonight. The idea of hearing a transvestite painted blue ranting about racial injustice is too much for me today. We can try tomorrow, if you like."

"I'm glad to have an evening with you."

"As long as you don't deconstruct it," Arlette smiled, for the first time that evening. "No grammar of story, if you know what I mean."

"What would a perfect evening together be? You tell me."

"I wish I knew. But imperfect is good enough. Only dinner. And a story or two. The usual back and forth."

"All right," said Jake. "You go first."

"O.K. I will. I wrote a poem today about why I can't write. Why I don't write. I brought it to read, just in case."

"Go ahead," he said. "And don't worry about whether or not it's good. Good doesn't matter. We both know that. It's arbitrary, anyway."

She felt her heart beat very loudly. Her hands were wet. Her throat seemed to swell. But she began to read, very carefully, very slowly, as though each word were an egg.

> For reasons of mothers
> and others
> mine

is a hamster life.
On a wheel
most of the time,
unable to stop
long enough
to tell you this story.
It was always summer
in my childhood.
Yellow beach,
big green house.
My whole life
right there.
Even love.
Twenty years later.
Another house.
Very small.
Twenty years
between
summers and stories.
No twenty-four hours
anywhere.
No children.
No histories.
No long
connected breathing
the way
yogis teach.
Only moments
here and there.
Standing
in suns.

She stopped reading, but didn't look up right away. She was a little afraid of Jake, afraid he would judge her by her poem, and not by her heart. That he would do what she did very often.

He spoke first. He was gentle with her, and she knew then that he might possibly love her. "So," he said very slowly. He looked at her with unmistakable kindness. Even more. "I liked your poem. Will you continue? Let me tell you a story now," he said. "Even though I'm not very good at stories."

"Good doesn't matter," she smiled.

"My father and mother didn't love each other," Jake began. Arlette's face was turned to him. She looked at him fully. "I don't know that either of them loved me. They were both so damaged by the war. They were in Poland. They've been afraid all their lives. It's hard for me to think about them. So I just don't. As a boy, I never knew much about where they were from. They didn't really want to say. Where they were born, who their parents were. I still know very little. I would ask sometimes, and they'd reply, 'Wait. Wait. Someday you'll know.' But I never did. They raised three children and sent us to college by working very hard. They never said a word. They both died as silently as they lived. It has taken me years and years to think about them, and their impact on my life. I guess their lives are part of my own."

"Thank you, Jake. You never quite said it that way before. It's so funny that we rarely discuss our past."

"That could be the only thing we have in common." He smiled, and it was hard for her to tell what he was thinking.

She laughed, and wondered if there was some truth to that.

"Now you," said Jake. "Say something. Anything."

"My real life began when I was eighteen. But my memories are from before. Those pictures that you hold in your head, bright red pictures full of smells and sounds, mine are all from childhood. But when I was able to leave my family, to go to college and hang paintings on a wall, to live in a world that had restaurants on the corner, and a park, and the promise of a broader life, then I felt as though I was finally beginning to live.

"My first day of college was one of those days you remember, and remember. My parents seemed relieved that I would be gone. I was not an easy child. They drove me to school, took me to dinner, and just drove away without the slightest drama. No tears. Only relief all around. In my room was a girl my age. She wore one long sausage curl hanging down the back of her head, to her waist. Her name was Divine, and she was from a religious family, from Baltimore, Maryland. She had a twin sister named Charity. I later found out it took hours to get that curl just to sit there the way it did. She was lost. What was funny was that I could feel how lost she was. And I who had never been in that city before felt very sure. I asked her to come out to dinner with me, and then I sat on a chair, and watched her get dressed. She wanted to change into a flowery skirt. I was wearing a black dress. My first. I didn't take it off, except when I had to. I loved that dress, and the life I expected to live in it.

"We went to a Vietnamese restaurant on our block. I had a noodle dish with bright green lines. They could have been coriander or cilantro, or spring onions. We sat there talking, and I remember thinking to myself that I had never been so happy. And that, in a way, was the beginning."

Slowly, they continued talking through the night. In and out, easy words, just like breathing.

5

dikran aram boyajian

Dear Miss Rosen: Should I call you Ms? That
doesn't make a lot of sense to me. Maybe it's my
generation (I'm 74) but I think either you're
married, or you're not. If you're married, it's
Mrs., and if not, it's Miss. What's so bad?

If you don't believe me that Miss is not
offensive, take a look at history. Not that
history's always right. I'll bet you'll find some
awfully successful Misses. Take a very close look.
Then you tell me. I'm waiting. You can let me know
what you find any time. And if you don't agree,
don't worry. I'm a mature man by now. I accept
disagreements. I even went once to couples
counseling.

So what's he writing about, I'll bet you're
wondering. And you're probably thinking to

yourself, a million to one he wrote a book. Well you're right, and you're wrong. I wrote the beginning. Not the whole book, because I don't know if it's of interest. If anyone's going to want to read it besides myself. That's an important question to know the answer to because if they don't, should I bother? Does a tree fall in the forest if there's no one around to hear it? My son, who told me about that tree, said yes, but I say no. You need an ear for sound. Otherwise it's nothing.

I wrote a book about God and the transmigration of ancient souls. You're probably thinking to yourself, now that's an unlikely subject for a 74-year-old man to write. Does he have any credentials? Did he study? And what can he possibly know?

All I have to say to that is a lot. I'll tell you the categories, and you tell me if I've covered the subject: Mercy and Love, Joy and Praise, People and God, Dignity and Responsibility, Integrity, Freedom, and Our Ancestors at the Gates of Heaven. And that's only Volume One (ha! ha!).

Are you interested? Tell me the truth. On the one hand, I think to myself "Who wouldn't be?" and on the other hand I think, "What am I, kidding?" You tell me. Of course I will pay for your opinion. You're a professional. I understand what that means. My children too. No opinions without money in advance. So how much?

Jack Green

Dear Jack Green, Who wouldn't be? What am I kidding? Or, OK I'll tell you. You can ask for my opinion. Send me the amount that you think your

book is worth. That's up to you. Is it a $5.00
book? $50.00? $500.00? How long is it, by the way?
I guess I'll see for myself, if you send it.
Arlette R.

Dear Arlette Rosen,

You've heard of any number of bizarre and unique
detectives, I'm sure. One-eyed, orchid-growing,
feminist, etc. I propose an Armenian mystery
series with Dikran Aram Boyajian as hero. He'd be
Dikran the Dick. His nickname's Deeke. A former
Orthodox priest, photo-engraver, opera singer, and
lighting designer, Dikran sells Oriental rugs. He
is short, dark, sexy, suave, and mustachioed. He
plays the oud and eats grape leaves twice a day.
He is divorced, because divorced detectives seem
to have more interesting sex lives. Using his
special skills as an Armenian, speaker of a unique
language unlike any other in the world, he
miraculously finds killers, in 30 days or less. He
has never failed. (By the way, none of the killers
are Turks. I want to avoid any kind of prejudice,
if I can.)

(Dikran is loosely based on an ex-husband of mine,
Dikran Latmanjian.) What do you think? Want to see
a sample of Dikran in Azerbajan? (Dikran in
Bimini, and Dikran in Crimea will follow.) These
are perfect holiday books. They are diverting, and
they don't bother anybody. I use descriptions of
foreign lands as often as I can.

Yours, VeeJee Smith

Dear VeeJee,

O.K. Send me Dikran. I think I like him. A. Rosen

Dear Arlette,

I'm writing to ask you for inspiration. Is it possible to send?

Here I sit, right on my balcony, which is approximately the size of two very small closets. No winter clothes. On a hazy Philadelphia morning. I can't see anything from here. The sky is eerie, the air is thick, and even the birds are silent.

I hope you are well. Do you remember that we met once? It was on a plane going to Chapel Hill, North Carolina. You were going to visit relatives. I was too. I'm writing to tell you that, as you suggested, I now write every day.

By the way, I'm sick. I have an awful cold, accompanied by bad sinuses, asthma, bronchitis, and general rhinitis. I didn't go to work for several days (I am a psychiatric social worker) and I didn't feel like seeing a doctor. I'm a little better now, but I'm still not inspired.

Writing is very, very hard. You didn't tell me that. I need a spark. Where does it come from? I can't just call it up. I have to wait for it to call me. Without this spark, my work is dead.

Maybe because I haven't felt well, I feel completely and totally uninspired. I want to write, but when I start, the words are just wrong. Emotion is missing. It's just an exercise. I am stuck.

Can you tell me how to unstick myself?

It was very kind of you to give me your address. I've been meaning to write for two years now. I held onto it. And now, I'm putting it to good use. I hope you haven't moved.

This being stuck happens to me in every area of my life, from child rearing and housework to making

love with my husband. I just have to wait it out.
Wait for that spark. Do you have any suggestions
in this regard?

I suppose I must just believe in the process, and
keep writing, knowing that it has to return. I'm
including a stamped self-addressed envelope, in
case you haven't saved my address.

Eileen Willis, MSW

Dear Eileen Willis,

I remember your bright pink jogging suit very
well. And I saved your recipe for peanut butter
pie. (But not your address, by the way.)

About inspiration, and being stuck, I absolutely
know what you mean. It comes and goes. Here's a
list of what I do, when I feel stuck. Which is
pretty often, by the way.

1. Walk in a circle seven times, counterclockwise.

2. Say the words "O Wa Ta Goo Siam" a few times,
very fast.

3. Lie on the floor. Palms up, head to one side,
knees bent apart. Legs open as wide as my hips. I
breathe very slowly, and imagine I am a bird.
Sometimes a tree is easier.

4. Sing. I don't know too many songs, so I usually
resort to a simple song from my childhood. "Row
Row Row Your Boat" or "Frere Jacques," or a Hebrew
school song like "Shalom Haverim."

5. Leave what I'm trying to do and do something
else. That's probably the best idea. At least I'm
not just sitting there frustrated. It seems
obvious and simple, but sometimes you have to
imagine a voice in your head saying, "Go outside."

43

6. Write the worst sentence you can think of. This often helps me. We live in fear of that sentence. How stupid and terrible it could possibly be. "It happened one cold night in a small town in Oklahoma." See? It's never really that bad.

7. Write a list. It doesn't matter about the subject. My own particular favorite is to write down the first ten words in your head. Keep these lists. They'll give you an idea of your moods. Sometimes, too, the words have stories in them.

8. Try to draw. This helps me because I am such a bad artist, I'm relieved to go back to language.

Good luck to you, Eileen. Don't stop. That's probably the best advice I can give. A.

6

my gorilla

Arlette and Jake decided to go away. Maybe in Puerto Rico, their lives could be different. They'd been there before, but never together. Jake liked Puerto Rico. He liked Latin music, loud engaging rhythms in the middle of nowhere, clubs and bars alongside the densest country road. Places where rhythms permeate each moment of daily life. Even the smallest towns had incredible musicians. Arlette liked the shade of green all over the island, dense rain forests, wet, heavy smells of wild ferns growing. Life in the streets. Tight clothes on so many very different bodies, making them all look ready.

They acted like nervous strangers together, on the plane—two people unsure of where they were going and why, who knew each other well enough for wariness. They were both polite, offering one another magazines, pillows, the window seat. They seemed awkward together, tentative and too careful. Even their conversation was stiff, almost formal. As familiar as they were with one another, they still remained distant, each of them holding back.

"Is there a film industry in Puerto Rico?" Arlette asked.

"I think so, yes. Someone at the Focus gave me the name of a documentary filmmaker in San Juan. He's done interesting work, and it may be appropriate for our festival on Caribbean culture," Jake replied.

"What else is in the festival?" Arlette continued, attempting to keep up her end. "I've got the program, if you'd like to see," Jake replied. Later, he too made similar forays.

"Have you come across any manuscripts on Puerto Rican politics?" he asked.

"Poster art," she replied. "I edited something on poster art once, which included some Puerto Ricans. It's a political art form, and most of the posters in the book were created to protest injustice of various kinds. They've got an impressive number of poster artists there." They each drank tropical coolers, tequila and fruits, and by the time they were ready to land, they were silent, holding hands.

"What would you like these four days to be?" Arlette asked Jake.

"I'd like us to try and enjoy ourselves. No more than that," Jake replied.

"I'd like that too," said Arlette.

The plane landed, and they continued talking, not as formally now.

"I'm thinking of starting to write a proposal for a documentary film about S. I. Newhouse. The mogul. It might be an interesting way of looking at media. Someone told me his motto was 'Speak Yiddish, dress British.' A good title for the film. Did I ever tell you about the first screenplay I ever wrote? My friend Alan Taft and I did it together. We called it *Gorilla*. It was kind of a traditional story. A man takes a trip to find his past. One of those childhood growing-up family-relationship stories, viewed in a seminostalgic semipastoral perspective, celebrating a more innocent past. You've seen a million of them. Anyway, throughout the story we planned on having gorillas just sitting around, or standing. The characters would walk by them, but nobody would say a word. They'd just be there. Everyone we showed the screenplay to said, 'Why Gorillas?' Can you believe that?"

"I can," she said. "There have to be reasons. Everyone wants reasons. Nothing can just happen. By the way, why were the gorillas there?" Then she laughed. "I'd like to start my novel, too. I really would."

"Then you will." The ride from the airport to the hotel was brief.

They'd reserved a room in a big, garish hotel with the kind of lobby that glittered. Mirrors everywhere, women flashing shiny red nails, men in sneakers, the well-heeled smell of French aftershave, and chocolate truffles. They arrived at noon, driving their rented car through an unexpected warmth, a deep wet warmth that seemed to seep through them even in the car. Jake drove, humming. Arlette looked out the window at traffic and trees, and she felt a little relieved. She saw a kind of fullness around her, a fullness she'd been missing. The earth looked as though it were growing.

Jake too felt happier. A little shyly, he held her loosely as they walked into their room. The room held the spare, anonymous blankness of many nondescript strangers. There was even a matchbook painting of a British ship at sea. The waves were blue meringues. Arlette held back a little when Jake very

47

slowly kissed her hair. When he moved to her eyes, she softened, though not altogether.

"What would you like here?" Jake asked her. "How can these four days help us?"

"I'd like to feel less lost," she said, "less small and useless."

"What about us?" he said. "Do you think we're at a point where who we are together should change?"

"I don't know what could," she said.

"I wonder," said Jake, and then he lifted her up all at once, and carried her outside where they made love on the balcony in the very warm air. They were gentle with one another, quietly grateful.

After a deep nap, they woke up together. "Jake," she said, when she was fully awake again. "I'd like to stay in the room for the rest of the day. Until dinner. I don't want to leave."

"I want to swim," he said. "To see the pool. Wouldn't you rather lie in the sun? After all, that's why we're here."

Jake put on his bathing suit very quickly. A small black square.

She did not answer him at first. She had come to Puerto Rico for different reasons than Jake. She wanted only to be together, in a way they normally weren't, to be alone in their room until they had no need to talk. She wanted to remove the distractions, to stay still. And she wanted to do this with Jake. After all this time, though, this was not something she could tell him. "I'd rather stay here." She tried not to sound childish.

"The beach is beautiful," he said. "The pool is part of a waterfall. I saw a picture. It falls from the top of a rock. You can sit under it and relax. And then sleep if you want, in a chair on the deck. You can hear the waves. We're on the ocean. It's surround sound right here."

Arlette, because she felt she didn't know how, could not fight back. "I'll see you in a while," she said. When he left, though, she began to resent him. She wanted someone who only wanted her.

But did she really? And if that's what she wanted, why was she with Jake? Jake was a person of boundaries. He had rules for keeping her away. Film was more important first of all. She felt like once she saw a problem, once she admitted to knowing it was real, she would really be forced to act. Where this idea came from was hard to say. Maybe in Puerto Rico, she'd be able to write a story, something more than a sentence or two, a story about Jerusalem. She'd been to Jerusalem half a dozen times. She'd lived there once for three months. Those months were caught inside her, like a very deep memory of shadows and sounds.

Jake left quickly. He carried a big black towel. Arlette put on her suit very slowly. In the mirror, she looked too fleshy, too white, ill-defined. Removed from sun. Her suit was a shiny purple bikini.

She bought it because it looked like something Jayne Mansfield might have worn, and although she herself was nothing like Jayne Mansfield, she liked the idea. As a child of eleven, she'd interviewed her once. Her family had been on vacation in the mountains. Jayne Mansfield and her husband, a handsome man named Mickey, had been there too. Arlette had thought about their bodies for months.

It was the first time she'd taken other people's bodies very seriously. The adults around her were far less fleshy, more powdered and hidden, more words than arms or legs. Their sex seemed caught up with language, and although she imagined them entwined together once in a while, it didn't seem central to their lives. Jayne and Mickey were all body. Arlette interviewed them for her grammar school paper. Together, they were her first official subject. She asked them about their favorite foods, their hobbies, their pets. She didn't know how to get any closer to their lives. She asked them to autograph a matchbook, and years later, she carried Jayne Mansfield's signature and her salutation, "For Arlette, a future bombshell," around with her like a good luck charm. Although the interview revealed no unusual information. Years later, Arlette still thought on occasion of those bodies, so luminous, so nearly naked, so full of life and excitement, more physically real in mysterious ways than anything else she'd ever known.

Jake, for all his seeming sureness, was always tentative with her, cautious, too controlled. When she thought of how they made love together, she thought about words. They were proper together, almost dutiful, acting in ways that seemed to be expected. Interested but not overly so. She decided to go out to Jake, to meet him, to take her notebook there.

The purple glitter of her bathing suit made her feel less tired. She wasn't angry when she saw Jake, or disappointed either. Only anxious, and a little uncertain about her own honesty with him. Jake whistled. "Jayne Mansfield?"

"Without the breasts," she replied.

"Jayne Mansfield if she'd read Philip Roth."

"Why Roth? I'm not altogether sure about him."

"I don't know why, but he seems to be a prerequisite for something or other. Don't ask me what. He's a signpost of something, like Yale Law School or Jesse Jackson. Do you think he's Woody Allen?

"Not at all," she said. "*The Ghostwriter* was a bad movie."

"Of course, but that's not Roth."

They continued in ways they knew how, until a tall, handsome man with bright blue eyes and a small white bathing suit stopped at their chair.

"New Yorkers?" he said. "Don't ask how I know. I'm psychic. Just a joke. I'm a painter, so I know what I'm looking at. I'll bet you're thinking to yourself, he means houses, right? That too. It's a good living. A few thousand dollars and a few cans of paint. Outsides are more. I'm a real painter though. Very real. Realistic in fact. I've got this particular scene, if you're interested. On rocks. That's the cheapest. Eight to twenty dollars." He smiled like a movie star. "I can put you in it too. That's extra. You in the pool. You in the ocean. You on vacation in Puerto Rico. Both of you'd be an additional five. A momento," he said. "You won't find another. John, by the way. I go by John. John DiGiorno." He shook their hands, like Burt Reynolds in Puerto Rico. A later Burt, still handsome. Arlette smiled back, but Jake did not.

"Do you have samples of your work?" she asked politely.

"Are you kidding?" he said. "Right in front of the hotel. There's a sidewalk craft show today. A lot of talent on display. You name it, we have it. I've got paintings on rocks, paintings on slate from a roof I fixed, paintings on beautiful grass cloth. A customer of mine threw it out. She's got money to burn. It was for her front hall. She said it looked like a golf course. She's nuts. Her husband's an executive for IBM, and you know the kind of money they make. I thought it would bubble. It doesn't. I put primer on everything first. That way, the paintings stay. It's better than a photograph. It's art. By the way, if you get nostalgic after a few days for some ski scenes, I have them too. They're a little more money. Skiers are at a premium here. I've seen a lot of them though. I come from Hunter, New York. A big mountain right there. The Sluskys own it. Nice people. They don't pay enough. That's how it is. My wife works in the ski shop in the winter. She skis herself. She's good. Six months here, six months there. Me too. Have paint will travel, you know what I mean. She pushes my rocks. Imagine this though. In the Hunter ski shop what goes is Puerto Rico. People. Who can figure. In the summer, it's all festivals. Irish, Italian, German, even Greek. They're all up there. I paint specialty rocks for each one. Shamrocks. Knockwurst. You name it, I paint it. Everyone loves them. They're universal. They are multicultural. You know how many I've sold already? Eight hundred and twelve. This winter, I'm going to break the thousand mark. Like McDonalds. So what do you say?"

"We're not interested."

"What about your wife? She seems eager."

"We're not married."

"Even better," he said. "Souvenir of an illicit trip. You'll want to remember this, believe me. After you're married, it all wears off. That's how it is. I know. They don't tell you that in the books. It's a well-known fact of life. Why do you think there are so many divorces? Someone else comes along and there it is again. The missing zing."

"That's a nice book title," said Arlette.

He smiled warmly. "Books," he said. "Boy do I have a story to tell. If you want it, be my guest. What I haven't seen isn't there. You can use it all. I don't have the time. It's just a question of sitting down. When I see you talking about the Missing Zing on TV, I'll be happy. Nice meeting you two. You decide on a rock, just look around," he said, and winked. "I'm not far away."

Arlette took out her small brown notebook. "Don't tell me you're writing him down," Jake said.

"Maybe," she said. "He would be an original character."

"I don't want to read about him. Ever."

But she played around with titles instead, in her notebook. Should *Jerusalem* be there or not? It might give the book too holy a feel. Not alive enough for what she wanted. She decided to add the weather later on, and begin anywhere. Maybe with the city.

She wrote in a small, neat hand, rarely crossing out words. With each sentence, she changed the color pen. She drew a picture, imprecise but clear, of hills and a palm tree, although she knew perfectly well there were no palms in Jerusalem. And she tried many names for her hero: Ahmed, Fuad, Fouzi, Agram, Adnan, and Feisel. As and Fs were all she could think of. She chose Ahmed because of the "ah." She thought the sound made him appear open. Ahmed entered. He walked like a man who knew what he was doing.

Jake floated in the water while Arlette wrote. Then he swam laps, long ovals around the pool, very smoothly, without stopping until he'd done one hundred even. Every once in a while, he looked up at Arlette. She looked mysterious and a little bit happier. For this, at least, Jake was glad. He took his time swimming to give her a chance, but after a while, he swam to her, sitting down carefully so as not to disturb her mood. Arlette looked up and smiled at him. "I've written a beginning of a story," she said. "I've set the stage. It's rough. It will probably change a hundred times. But I've started," she said. "I want to read you this poem I found stuck in a book. I wrote it a while ago. The second poem in a month. I want you to hear it, though you might not like it. It isn't clever, or modern. It has none of the traits you admire."

"I'd like to hear it, no matter what," he said.

She began to read very slowly, shyly, as though he were a stranger. "It's called 'Tell Me a Story.'"

> This is my life.
> These words
> This room

This poem
Some bright colored days.
Sentences:
Tell me a story.
I will tell you a story.
Once there was
and once there wasn't.
A long time ago
in a small town
in Bupst, there lived
an old man
an old woman.
Then they were young.
One day, he told her
he loved her.
And then he left.
All her life, she told
this story.
Sometimes she
changed
the ending.

"How could I not like that?" he said. "Of course I do. Absolutely."

"Now will you read the very beginning of *Jerusalem*? Maybe I should call it *Souk*. Do you think that's too cliched? It doesn't matter what I call it."

"Do you really want me to?"

"I'm not sure," she said. "Yes and no, but maybe more yes. I guess so."

"Would you like to tell me the plot? Because if it's one of those Romeo and Juliet stories, I might react badly. You know. Black woman, white man. Vice versa. Arab. Jew.

Mombar. Mindy. It just seems so pointed, you know. We should all get along, each tribe is the same. Mohammed and Moses both begin with M. The kind of reductionism that turns the world into a Coke commercial. If that's not what you're doing, then maybe I should read it. It's up to you."

"Who's hostile now?" she said. "What's your problem? You've been working on a screenplay for years. Would I ever reduce it to a buddy movie? It's all how the story is told. Are you angry with me about something?"

Jake was silent. Then he looked up.

"I suppose I am," he said. "You've been very remote, and I don't know why. You're somewhere else. I resent it. You've been hard to reach." Arlette sighed, but she didn't interrupt. "I suppose in the beginning that was the basis for our relationship—we were both pretty unreachable. But we've been together for three years now. And we're still so careful with one another. Why do we continue to stay together? Is it apathy, or hope? We don't make enough demands of each other. Without demands, I'm not sure what goes on is very real." His voice became louder, more forceful.

"How could we be different together?" she said, a little too softly. "I don't have the answer. It's not a formula we're looking for, but a way to feel closer, happier."

"Is that possible?"

Arlette looked at Jake. His body seemed less frail. His black bathing suit shined. He was stretched out on the chair besides her. A copy of a large book about Orson Welles was open beside his chair. She wanted him, she knew that much was true. Though she wasn't quite sure what *wanted* really meant.

"I wish you'd read poems," she said. "Any poems. Even Wallace Stevens. Or Poe. I read once that most men like Poe. Is that true?"

"You're so impossible. Would I be a better person if I read poetry? I don't think so. We both might be better if we'd go for a swim. Right now. You and me. No thinking. No words. Just gliding through artificial blueness. Come on Arlette. You're Jayne Mansfield. I'll be whatshisname. What is it, by the way?"

"Mickey Hargitay." He stood up and so did she. He pinched her ass and she jumped into the pool, a momentary swan, finally laughing. They stayed in the pool for hours.

7

what harbinger says

Dear Miss Rosen,

I have considered your offer with the seriousness it deserves, and although my initial reaction was less than enthusiastic to the idea of your fee and mine being equivalent, I have come to reconsider. Why should taxes have more value than the human soul? Which we both agree is the essence of writing, I'm sure. I discussed this matter with several of my colleagues, including a Dr. Malachy, who teaches an excellent course in ethics at Fordham University, a course I myself have audited on more than one occasion. Should you have the opportunity, I recommend this highly. It's Tuesday evenings at 8. Dr. Malachy is a very intelligent man. There isn't much he hasn't considered. I posed the question to him this way (I thought you might be interested): "Would you say that one profession is worth more than another?" And then I offered him the specific example of equating your book doctoring job with mine. His response was that the idea was an interesting one. Worth testing. He has asked me to offer the results to him first. He thought perhaps this idea might be worth a paper. Brief perhaps, but probably publishable. Law journals abound. I accept your interesting offer, with pleasure and expectation. By the way, I have worked carefully on my opening sentence. It may be this: Marla and Eqbal seethed. (Seethed together? Happily seethed?) Either that, or Marla and Eqbal were a seething pair. What do you think? You will tell me, I presume, at our first official consultation, where I pay. Yours in expected admiration,

Harbinger Singh

Dear Harbinger Singh,

I'm glad you both found my arrangement ethically acceptable.

Money is one of those difficult subjects. God knows there have been enough books about it. I look forward to your appointment, and our work together. Yours, AR

To: A. Rosen

From: P. DeSapio
Re: *Otto and Me: The True Story of My Happy Marriage (to a Gorilla)*

In a private ceremony two years ago performed by an Ethical Cultural Official, I married a male gorilla named Otto. After 24 months of much happiness and considerable excitement, I've decided to go public with our story, in hopes that it will encourage others involved in human-animal bonds not to have to keep them secret.

I am chief legal counsel for Consolidated Edison.
They thought I was single, until last Christmas,
when I showed up at the party with Otto. Our life,
and the reactions of others to it, is what I'd
like to share, with your help.

Although there are gorilla books galore, and we
have them, I believe this is the first public
portrait of a successful modern interspecies
marriage, human and gorilla.

My outline's in three parts:
1. The Meeting
2. The Marriage
3. Now

I address many issues, including our differences,
reactions of family and friends, religion,
children, money, sex, home life, and recreation.
Would you like to see it? I need some advice about
tone.

I'd like the reader to identify with us, and am
not sure how to do that.

FINALLY, I MADE IT!

DEAR MRS. ROSEN,

FINALLY, I MADE IT! REPRESENTS A LOT OF WORK ON MY
PART. YEARS. I'VE GOTTEN 35 REJECTIONS FROM
PUBLISHERS WHO DON'T UNDERSTAND THEIR OWN MARKET.
IT'S BIG. BELIEVE ME, I KNOW QUITE A FEW PEOPLE
WHO ARE WAITING FOR THIS BOOK. IT'S ALL TRUE.
EVERY WORD. A FRIEND SUGGESTED, A DR. WARNICK,
THAT MAYBE YOU KNOW A WAY TO MAKE IT A LITTLE
SMOOTHER. YOU HELPED HIM TWO YEARS AGO. IT'S THE
STORY OF A JOURNEY FROM AUSCHWITZ TO HOLLYWOOD, A
JEWISH HORATIO ALGER STORY. LEE IACOCCA, IF YOU
LIKE THAT BETTER. IT TELLS MY OWN HARROWING
HISTORY, MY BOUTS WITH LIFE, WITH SICKNESS, WITH

TWO LOVELY WIVES, SELMA AND MICHELLE, AND MY THREE
SONS, ALL VERY SUCCESSFUL. BOOKS THEMSELVES.

THE FOREWORD IS BY ELIE WIESEL. I KNOW HIM
PERSONALLY. ONCE WE WERE ON A PODIUM TOGETHER, AND
SPEAKING FRANKLY, I WAS BETTER. BELIEVE ME. BUT
HE'S A GENIUS. THERE'S NO DENYING THAT. SOMEONE
SAID HE DREAMS IN POEMS. CAN YOU IMAGINE? AND
AFTER ALL HE'S BEEN THROUGH.

I CAN PAY YOU WELL FOR YOUR WORK. BUT RIGHT NOW. I
NEED IT YESTERDAY. I DON'T HAVE FOREVER. I'M NOT
GETTING YOUNGER. (YOU'RE PROBABLY NOT, EITHER.)

YOURS DEVOTEDLY, JACK GREENBERG

8

la hacienda

After their swim, after drinks by the pool and a walk on the beach, they returned to the room to nap before dinner. The room looked more familiar the second time, still dark, cool, as empty as a cocoon missing its butterfly.

Jake took a shower, and came out wrapped in a small white towel. The shades were drawn, and Arlette turned on a light by the bed to read. She always carried books with her: a volume of poems, a novel, a third book she'd always intended to read but knew she never would, like *Bullfinch's Mythology* or *Magic Mountain*. Jake, when they traveled, took one book and he read it. They did not read out loud to each other, or talk very much about their reading, although on occasion, Jake might ask Arlette to explain why she read all the time, and Arlette, defensive, might say that it was better than sitting in a dark room every day, just watching.

"I wish you'd read something to me," Jake said, not coming straight to her bed but sitting in a hotel chair, right next to the round breakfast table in front of the window. The blinds were drawn, and Jake did not turn on the light in the corner. "Anything. It doesn't matter. Even a poem. Go ahead."

"This is from a story by E. M. Forster. It's the opening paragraph of *The Machine Stops*. You've seen films from his books: *Howard's End*, and *A Passage to India*. Here's a paragraph that might be good to read in this room. It's the opening of a story."

> Imagine, if you can, a small room, hexagonal in shape, like the cell of a bee. It is lighted neither by window nor by lamp, yet it is filled with a soft radiance. There are no apertures for ventilation, yet the air is fresh. There are no musical instruments, and yet, at the moment that my mediation opens, this room is throbbing with melodious sounds. An arm-chair is in the centre, by its side a reading desk—that is all the furniture. And in the arm-chair there sits a swaddled lump of flesh—a woman about five feet high, with a face as white as a fungus. It is to her that the little room belongs.
>
> An electric bell rang.
>
> The woman touched a switch and the music was silent.
>
> "I suppose I must see who it is," she thought, and set her chair in motion.

"I liked it," said Jake. "That's all. A very graceful beginning."

"I wonder why you're so interested. You never seemed to be before. Is it me? I wonder if I read all the time to keep you away. But you're not the only reason. I love to read. Love the endless stories. I like the hopefulness in stories, the romance and wariness and all the narrative past. What we remember, and how those memories become who we are. Years ago I found a quote from a wonderful rabbi, Abraham Heschel. Have you ever heard of him? He was a scholar, a mystic, and an activist. He said, 'There is no human being who does not carry a treasure in his soul; a moment of insight, a memory of love, a dream of excellence, a call to worship.' For me, that's what writing really is. Any writing. And maybe filming too. They are prayers. Do you agree?"

"Of course," he said. "Come here."

They seemed to get closer together in the room, although the air remained too cold, the darkness too constant. A hum persisted, a light bulb or an air conditioner or something in the bathroom, a refrigerator hum that seemed close to a song. The room felt as though they were nearly somewhere else, almost another country, a place separate enough and foreign enough where nothing too serious was real, where the world disappeared into hot days and drinks by the pool, with strangers who had lives with no bearing on theirs, doing nothing more serious than turning darker shades. A place where loving each other was easier.

They pushed the beds together. Arlette rolled over onto Jake, naked and smooth, waiting for her. The color he sometimes became. Deep yellow. She felt herself opening onto him. Jake inside her. She inside Jake.

"Jake," she whispered. "It's very difficult to say anything at all." He looked at her with kindness, and with love. "Only Arlette," is all he replied.

Afterwards, while Arlette slept, Jake looked through the hotel guidebook for the restaurant that someone at the Focus had mentioned. He walked around the room first, straightening the dresser, closing the blinds even more tightly, turning off the light near Arlette's bed. Jake envied her easy sleep. She looked beautiful in bed, untroubled and ageless, and Jake suddenly felt how unhappy he'd be if she ever left him. He sometimes knew that what he wanted was not simple: to be Jean Luc Godard, or even Alfred Hitchcock, to make films instead of watching them, to take a chance and leap into darkness with a camera. He knew how easy it was to fail, to be criticized by others who thought criticism was their due.

He liked his work, liked his days spent with people who took movies as seriously as he did. Still he knew this alone would never be enough. He hoped his screenplay, a story he'd been thinking about for years, would help. But sometimes he felt like Jack Nicholson in *The Shining,* typing the same sentence over and over again. Only crazy.

He worked very little on his screenplay, although he often sat in a room alone with his few acceptable pages, fumbling through them, making changes here and there. It was easy, really, to change what he had written. Over and over again.

He saw everything as material. On occasion he'd cut stories of atrocities out of the paper, facts about injustice he happened to read. He knew for instance that there were thirty-five major civil wars happening in the world. He intended to use this, somehow.

His own story was about the myth of manhood through a bisexual love story in Ibiza that ended with death. In his outlines, and he'd written many over the years, he played with having everyone die all at once. He'd also tried each of the characters in turn. But nothing really worked in a satisfying way. He often changed the title, hoping to change his subject in that way,

He waited for Arlette to wake up on her own. He did not wake her, did not want to, either. He picked up a book next to her, pulling out two letters stuck inside.

He began reading them right away. All the letters were like insistent voices, funny whispering ambitious sounds from strangers who told their secrets. Other people who very briefly were there within her life. He liked the letters as much as she did.

Dear A.

I want to write a book called *Psychic Exercises*: Ways of stretching your mind (back and forth, up and down, in and out).

I can do yours free, as a gift, so you can see it works.

What is your very honest reaction?

O.O.
c/o The Very Open Center
Rye, New York 10580

Dear Rose Rosen,

Chi Fang and Dr. Tybellay Htlueby gave me your name and address. I am interested in writing a scholarly book that would interest the general public nonetheless (I would write it clearly, in an accessible manner) on a most timely subject, namely Multiculturalism: The Debate. To be honest, I think it presents a very mixed blessing. For the first time we are being given voices we have not heard before. As you know, we here in America live in a society that declares itself pluralistic, but throughout this country's history (and here, I might add for the sake of fairness, in most of the history of much of the world) we have heard one single voice. It is white, male, and Western European. This voice certainly does not speak for most of us. But there is a danger, too. The danger

is that multiculturalism runs a risk of becoming
on the one hand an emotionally separatist cultural
movement, and this itself will make us self-
conscious. It will place us in the box we're
allotted. Many of us are concerned with universal
themes, themes which transcend ethnicity or
nationality. Love, loyalty, morality, honor,
betrayal, peace, etcetera.

I would like to write about this new multicultural
fascination (it is even in *Independence Day*) with
a clear eye, an eye that is, by the way, both
Chinese and Jewish. I myself am a lesbian academic
(a professor of feminist sociology, with an avid
interest in many subjects, multi-cultural and
otherwise.) My list of published works is
enclosed. I've just completed an extensive review
of the novels of Japanese writer Kazuo Ishiguro, a
genius. He is, as you know, both British and, of
course, Japanese. So you see, my work is not
restricted to women.

I understand you can help. I need some aid, though
perhaps not all that much, with liveliness. My
friends tell me you are very lively, and are good
at the task of enlivening texts. What does that
mean, exactly? How much money is involved?
Although I am successful, my success is not
measured in money. I'm sure you understand.

I am eager for your affirmative and encouraging
reply. (I speak several languages.)

Ciao, Shalom, and Hasta la Vista,

Xi Yen Rosenberg

Jake sat watching her sleep for a while. Just watching.
What he saw was someone he very deeply loved. She woke
up very suddenly. "Jake, Jake, Jake," she said, and looked at
him intently. The room was still dark. "I'd like to explain.

66

But I don't think I can. My explanations would be a lifetime of stories. I don't know any other way. I can tell stories. That's all. You like the dark, and stories. You like them better on the screen. That's all."

Jake moved into the bed beside her. He held onto her loosely, and started to sing. "You are my sunshine. My only sunshine." He sang all the verses he knew. They held one another until it was time to leave for dinner.

Their days in Puerto Rico were full of the white yellowish glow, the kind of glow that is around Puerto Rican beach towns. It's the color of bananas on trees in very early morning. Every night, they sat in open bars facing water, looking at small blue pieces of ocean littered with tense bodies trying to relax by jumping up and down, then lying still. They often sat not quite facing each other, but still together the way some people are. Not so obviously intertwined, with the desperation of some kinds of lovers, but tied together with a more invisible fabric, a gauze of loose transparent fibers, made out of a more elusive thread. They left loosely holding hands.

9

live client

Ingeborg Kulka was a woman of seventy, still beautiful, still confident in a worldly way that made it seem as if what she wanted could be hers. Arlette, at Ingeborg's request, met her in a coffee shop, a New York version of Vienna on Seventieth and Broadway. The room was large and subtle, with light orange walls, and Mozart on tape.All the cakes were named after composers.Bach and Beethoven were chocolate and vanilla. Each had their own variations, their own shelves, pastries named for major works.

The people in the room looked serious, as though they were almost in Europe. Everyone seemed in the middle of an intense discussion of something very worthy: apartheid, injustice, religion, a poem. Ingeborg got in touch with Arlette through a psychiatrist whose book Arlette had worked on, a novel about a psychotic killer with an IQ of 170, called Mental Giant. The psychiatrist did well with his novel. He'd thanked Arlette profusely, even giving her a leather-bound copy. Ingeborg Kulka was his patient.

Arlette liked to be the person who waited, so she got to the coffee shop early. Ingeborg was easy to spot. She carried herself like a Viennese lady, elegant, careful, neat in a way that seemed more artistic than cautious. She wore a tomato silk blouse, a red that made her skin look creamy white, and long earrings, sculpted silver drops that looked more like Henry Moore than Mexico. She held her head so straight it almost seemed as though a weight was dropped through the top of her body straight down the center. Even so, she was not like a dancer, not like someone whose steps were choreographed by someone else.

Arlette sat up a little straighter. She was wearing white, and wondered very briefly if she looked a little too nurselike, when that was not her intention. At her best, she looked like a cross between Primo Levi, Mick Jagger, and Cher. Sometimes she worried that she looked a little too much like a Jewish woman from Westchester who'd once had an affair with a Quiche Indian and never forgot those wild three days, the kind of wide-hipped woman who discusses estrogen and only wears silver bangles.

"I am Ingeborg Kulka," said the beautiful stranger, as gracious as though she were greeting a dignitary. "I am terribly pleased that we can at last have this chance to meet. The references you have are very strong. I am encouraged by that. It speaks well of my own chances."

"What are you writing?" Arlette knew by now that talking about other things was not what anyone wanted.

"Written," she said. "The writing has already taken place. For the most part. I need help knowing what went wrong, and how I can somehow fix it. I am now at a loss, although I have finished two novels. I am a painter, you see, and more comfortable with visual imagery. But the stories could only be told in this very way. I am certain of that. They are true stories, of course, though I suppose everyone's novels are true. Or are they?"

"It depends," said Arlette. "Although if a story's not true, it doesn't seem to matter very much. Some people write novels, maybe men more than women, that are constructs really, verbal chess games. More cleverness than truth. Those books don't interest me very much."

"My book is all truth entirely," Ingeborg said. "My mother was a prostitute in the camps. She was very beautiful, and, in fact, she had no choice. It was that or die. She fell in love with a German Army officer, and he with her. He was my father." Ingeborg's face, full of a dignity that comes from having seen tragedy and survived, was all emotion, a sad soft moon. Her eyes filled easily, and Arlette envied her that.

"Then he left," she continued. "He found her Jewishness unbearable, or so she explained to me. I believed her though, because I never saw my father again, and my only memory of him is from photographs. Oddly enough, I remember his feet, and the boots he seemed to wear all the time. I have never been able to bear my husband's wearing boots. He's a survivor too, and he understands this kind of behavior."

"What happened to your mother?" Arlette spoke very softly.

"My mother tells you what happened, in my novel. The story is actually told from her perspective, and not from the child's," she replied.

"What made you do that?"

"Hers is the more compelling story," she replied. "Although I was in a kind of prison with my mother, a prison from which I saw no escape, not so much as a door to unlock, or a path that could lead me away, still my life would always hold a lesser kind of sadness, not as tragic, not as full, not as interesting a story. I would never be as beautiful, nor would I have the same terrible choices. My life is not even a shadow of hers," she said. "When he left, she thought of herself as fallen. Her family had been cultured, wealthy, and highborn. They were Jews, but they were also Germans, methodical, well placed in the world or so they thought. They were sure their own logic along with their cleverness would save them. They did not understand irrationality. Theirs was an ordered world of knowledge and precision, of art in its place, and purposeful order, of careful forays into rational arenas. And then it fell apart."

Arlette stopped Ingeborg Kulka. "Should we order?" she asked. "Not yet, not yet." And then she continued her story.

"She fell in love again, my mother, this time with a woman. A woman who taught karate. Her name was Olga. My mother took karate because she felt weak, and Olga gave her muscles. They adopted a child, my half-brother Paul. He is ten years younger than I am, though his life was very different. His story is in my second book." She smiled the knowing smile of an author whose story is her life. "He's black," she said. "Though I suppose these days you say Afro-American. Afro-German, maybe. He had a Bar Mitzvah, though. Both my mother and her lover chose to be Jewish. There's a story there too. This is all true, of course. But I've written it as a novel. I've decided to write this as fiction, in part because all the facts are not really known to me." Here she smiled, a peculiar smile impossible to interpret. "I've brought you the first manuscript, which is somewhat long. But you'll see. It's eighty-four thousand words," she said. "More or less. If you want to read the continuing saga, just let me know. I am home most of the time. I am working on a painting series, called Mornings in the Camps. It's light and darkness. That's what I'm trying for. And if you can figure out what the matter is here, I'll be very grateful to you. It's stiffer than I'd like," she said. "The story itself is not a stiff one. It's difficult though. Large themes, set against a kind of dailiness. But I'm sure you are familiar with these problems."

"Yes," said Arlette, who knew that the woman herself was more interesting than her book. "I'm looking forward to reading this," she said, although she only half meant it. And Ingeborg smiled more broadly.

"Money," said Ingeborg. "Shall we discuss this? Or not. I prefer not to, if you don't mind. Just give me a bill with your written evaluation. And I will pay it promptly. I have inherited that capacity, along with the rest. Now, perhaps we should have a brief conversation. Would you like to tell me about yourself?"

"Not particularly."

"Just something. It doesn't matter what."

"I am a Leo. A double Leo. My birthday is in August. I collect handwriting in many forms: author's query letters, Christmas letters, postcard messages, shopping lists, autograph books. I like to save the handwriting of strangers. I'm as interested in how it looks as what it says. Sometimes I hang their notes on the wall. I have always looked at handwriting as its own art form. It seems very personal, more evocative even than photos. Handwriting reminds me of listening to the radio, where you hear the timber of the voice, and only imagine the rest."

"I believe I see," said Ingeborg Kulka, nodding.

After Ingeborg Kulka left, Arlette remained in the café. She listened around her, and drank her coffee. It was a nice enough room, the kind of room where sitting was very easy. She took out her notebook to record her impressions of Ingeborg Kulka, to put into a file.

I liked her, and I didn't, she wrote. *Her story of course incredible. Large. Dramatic. Impossible. Unexpected. How did her story shape her own life?* Arlette sat in the café for a while. An hour more. Maybe even two. She ordered another pot of espresso, and drank it very slowly, happy to be alone in a full room, with her notebook.

Before she left, she read a letter. It was in a white number ten envelope with a Columbia University insignia. It was all typed, very official. She guessed from the envelope that the book would be dry. But she'd been wrong before.

```
Dear Arlette Rosen, B.D.,

I understand from Professor Adorno at Columbia
that you are very interested in ideas of all
kinds, and in the process of turning them to
books. I am too. In fact, I've written a book of
ideas, which stems out of my lifelong pursuit: a
good biography, at long last, of Martin Buber.
(Did you know, by the way, that in Jerusalem, his
city, there isn't even a street in his name? Can
you imagine?)

The following paragraph is more or less the
summary statement of my thesis. I have worked on
this forever. It suffers somewhat from the
language of my discipline. I am the Moses
Maimonides Professor of Jewish History, Culture,
Society, and Politics at Louisiana State
University.
```

Beneath Buber's metamorphosed cabalism, and his somewhat heterodox Marxism (was he a Marxist after all?), one senses a primal intuitive vision. He had a very early desire to reveal the link between language and all things, of beings and God, and of cultural and material superstructures. In my book, *Martin Buber: The Man,* I attempt (given that the barriers between German, Hebrew, and English are insurmountable) to explain him, his confrontation with Zionism, Hasidism, and morality, and his love life. We follow his moods, his ideas, the genesis and development of his major works, and his marvelous and disturbing life.

I know there are many people out there, in the United States as well as in Israel, Europe, and other places, that have been waiting for a final definitive Buber work. I believe this could be what they're waiting for.

However, it suffers from being a little too elusive. Too hard to follow. While the larger archetypal patterns may be present, it still gets lost. I want to make it clearer, and need your help.

My good friend Dr. Adorno says you are a word surgeon. You go right in there and remove the linguistic cancer. Is that true? I believe I have a malignant case. My wife calls it "word disease." Are you the appropriate healer? Help me if you can. It's for a good and noble cause.

Yehuda Weinreich Mizner, PhD

Arlette still sat at the table, thinking about Ingeborg Kulka, and Martin Buber, and even Harbinger Singh. Why was he different from the rest? Or, was he?

10

mosesjacobmoon

All morning, Arlette imagined Harbinger's arrival. She again tried not to consider his profession as a strike against him. Or his brown wool suit in summer, or the naive, florid way he talked about his writing. She tended to be more susceptible to writers who quoted Rilke, and mentioned seeking truth. Writers who quoted Gertrude Stein, or Virginia Woolf, or the Russians. Writers who talked about Borges or Eliot or Proust.

Harbinger Singh was not like that. He reminded her of Stan Markowitz, a travel writer she'd worked with once, who'd written a guide to Egypt. He was thin and fussy, rating Egyptian weather and people and hotels as though they were all restaurants, he the critical and eternally disappointed diner. Egypt, it seemed, did not live up to his standards, though nothing else did either. His book did well, and he ended up writing a whole series that he called The Only Truly Truthful Guides to the World. He sent the published books to Arlette with identical notes that read, "another Markowitz corner of the world."

Harbinger Singh was different from Stan Markowitz. He seemed more poignant in spite of his presumptuous ways. That he wanted to write a book was nothing surprising. That he believed it was as simple as taxes was more of a problem. She wished he were more riddled with self-doubt. Sometimes she thought that her connection to Jake was based on a sense of hopelessness, a knowledge that neither of them would ever do much of anything. On good days, she labeled this existentialism. Or Zen. Most of the time, however, she knew it was a kind of impossible passivity, a kind of inaction that was very hard to change.

Sometimes, usually when she was taking a bath—maybe it was the hot water—she wished she herself could write the very kind of big book that Harbinger described. Long and dense and full, ripe with wet sex scenes and a murder or two.

Or pick a subject, any subject, like most of her writers seemed to do—capital punishment, or crime, or male menopause—and define it in an interesting way. She wished there was something she knew well enough to explain. Some concept or phenomenon, some issue or cultural bias, some small part of dailiness.

Harbinger Singh rapped loudly on her door. "Hello," he shouted, in a loud, familiar way. She wondered what Carla was like, and why he loved her. She somehow knew he did.

"Ms. Rosen," he spoke clearly. "Singh is right here."

"I've brought you some potato candy," he said when she opened her door. "I know that is not very professional of me. Certainly not lawyerly either. Imagine offering a judge, for instance, some candy. Or an auditor downtown. Not that you are a judge. Although I suppose it is not unlikely to assume that your profession requires some judgment. In a way, you are judging my prose. Or are you? You might feel more comfortable denying that aspect of this process. Our relationship-to-be might be a more honest way of phrasing it. Please. The candy is delicious. The texture may seem wrong at first. Your American candy is harder. Someone told me, an unpleasant client I had the misfortune of representing once, that potato candy tasted like sweet white mud. I didn't understand this. What could she have meant? White sand turns brown. We all know that. Perhaps she was amplifying her own unpleasantness. She had to pay thousands. For once, it seemed a just reward. Impossibly unpleasant individual. You have those sometimes. You must too, I am sure. All of us in the service business suffer together. Often in silence, isn't that true?"

Arlette listened carefully to his nervous rambling. She couldn't help but wonder what it was she found so compelling. His words? His delivery? Both?

"How are you, Ms. Rosen? May I call you Arlette? If we are to be professionally reciprocal, I can tell you that I do on occasion allow certain clients to use my first name. I would allow you that privilege, for instance. Don't ask me why. It's an instinct I have. On occasion, I use my instincts to guide me. Though not often. I am guided by my rational self. Un-Eastern, in that way." He smiled.

"How are you, Arlette? There. Is that better? You may not want to tell me. After all, we are truly strangers. You can give me an answer in passing. The sky is blue today sort of remark. I myself am relatively well," he added, and took a loud, deep breath. He sounded as though he were gulping underwater.

"Of course that is one of the phrases I use far too often. It may be meaningless. I don't have enough skill or access with ways of more accurately describing my various states. Perhaps you can help me." He gulped again and looked up, as though he were closely examining her ceiling.

"Thank you for your candy," she said. "I have actually seen it, though I've never eaten it before. Did you have a beard when you were last here? I know it's impossible for someone to grow a beard in that short a time, but I don't remember yours. Please do come in," she said.

He moved behind her through her narrow hallway, following her into the living room. He sat down in the middle of her pinkish velvet couch, all anticipation. "These books," he said, pointing at the shelves. "An appropriate deduction. Have you actually read them? Don't be afraid of the IRS in your answer. We are in total confidence here. How many are there, do you suppose? I am better at estimating the size of crowds." He smiled as though she were visiting him. "Yes, I did have a beard, by the way. This one exactly. Though I vary my facial hair often. A moustache. A beard. Hairlessness too. Though I don't particularly like my chin. It is slightly weak. Could I control that, it would be strong and square. Germanic, perhaps.

"I have even had ponytails on occasion. More stockbroker than bicycler, I'm afraid. I do like hair however. It is a subject I know well. My greater family has an abundance. My father, who is now 104, has hair that goes underneath both his feet. And he is a very tall man. Believe me. I know you think of us as small brown people. Raisinlike. Untrue."

He continued nervously, and she couldn't tell if it was because he wanted her to know about him, or if he was just too nervous for silence.

"Some of my family are Sikhs," he went on. "Our body hair is sacred. I am not a Sikh. Not at all. I'm a Marxist. Don't be surprised. I can almost anticipate your response. Taxes and Marx, aha. That response is not uncommon, although these days, there is yet another reaction. Just plain Marx, aha. Still none of us are simple people."

She did not reply right away. There was silence between them. And then she said, "I know that. When I first began working with authors, I was really impressed with their endless resourcefulness. People want to write about everything: their great Aunt Margery and the time she hitchhiked across America to see a boy she'd loved in high school, ways they knew for removing gum from a thousand difficult places, plans for peace in Ireland, cookbooks with ginger ale as the primary ingredient. You wouldn't believe what I've seen," she said. "Some of these books find audiences. I actually see them in stores. I had a proposal once called *How to Juggle with What's Around Your House*. You wouldn't believe how many that's sold."

"So you're not particularly put off by my reference to Marx," he said. "Though let me reassure you, if you should have any qualms. The application in my life is not large."

"I'm put off by taxes, not Marx," she said.

"Why is that? And by the way, is the clock ticking? Because if it is, if I am paying for us to discuss why taxes might disturb you, I'd like to change the subject. I'm sure you understand. While the answer might in some way be beneficial to my writing, or even my life, it's a rather circumspect approach, and I am interested in moving forward on my novel of revenge. I do, however, want to know your opinion on this subject, which could be useful in other regards. So if you don't mind answering my question about the clock, we'll have a better idea on how we might proceed. A client once compared tax preparation to endodontia. He told me about a survey done where five hundred people were asked which they preferred: doing their taxes or having a root canal. Most picked taxes, by the way."

"I would too. The clock's not ticking. It's not on right now. I don't work that way exactly. There's a clock, but it's imprecise. We'll begin in a minute. Taxes just seem dull, but I may be missing the 'it's one of those unchanging jobs that people just do' factor. Jobs you can better understand if the worker has no choice. But you picked it," she said. "It was what you decided to do. Your choice."

"I see you don't understand the metaphor of taxes," he said. "In fact, it is apparent. Personal taxes are portraits of the soul: philanthropy, spirit, psychological well-being are all reflected in where your money goes. Corporate taxes are another matter. Far more complicated. Perhaps if we get to know one another better," he said, drifting off a little. He smiled at her, a smile that was hard to read. She changed the subject.

"I worked with a dentist once who told me that teeth were like rings on a tree," she said. "Her book was good. I was surprised. It's funny how some people look interesting, as though the story they could tell might be full of whistles and crevices, while others look dull, like their stories would have to be wooden. In the end you can't tell. It's like sex partners, I guess."

He looked surprised, but asked very quickly, "Have you had many?"

"*Many* is one of those words," she said. "like *beautiful* or *tall*. Maybe," she smiled at him warmly," but that too is irrelevant to your novel. Let's begin. You seem ready. I don't talk about sex or religion, by the way. Only mine. Yours is no problem. It's just policy."

Harbinger took a yellow legal pad out from his Samsonite briefcase. His writing on the pad was dark and small, like locusts. "Shall I begin?" he said. "Or is there a more ritualistic way to proceed? Perhaps you should hum."

"Hum?" she said. "What?"

"We'd have to think of an appropriate song to accompany my text," he suggested, half smiling.

"For next time. That can be one of your assignments."

"No, I'm ready to suggest 'Love Me Tender' by Elvis Presley for today. You can consider that," he said. "I have titled this section 'Incipient Passions,' or 'A Stallion at the Gate.' 'Love Me Tender' would be appropriate, but we'll consider that for next time too. It can be the novel's theme song," he said, smiling broadly now.

He leaned back into the couch and crossed his legs, swinging them carelessly. His voice dropped an octave as he started to read.

> Eqbal and Marla seethed. Their seething was a critical part of their relationship, the centerpiece. This was not apparent in other parts of their lives. She tied him to their bed each night with periwinkle blue scarves. The bed itself was brass.

"Stop there." Arlette started to laugh. This threw Harbinger off for a minute. But he quickly regained his composure.

"Why?" he said. "I am only beginning here. I thought a sex scene was a good way into a novel. You'd want to keep reading. People have done it before. What could be more interesting than their sex life? A murder, maybe. Sex will make you want to learn more about them. Anyone who has a sex life is already interesting."

He smiled nicely.

"But we don't know Eqbal or Marla, or why they are seething. We don't know how tall they are, what they think and do, where they live, what their lives were like before and after their seething. What they eat and think and believe. What they look like. The color and shape of their eyes. How much they sleep. Who their friends are. Where they come from. What happened before the novel began. We have to see them first, to have some idea who they are. Where they come from. What's inside."

"Why?" he said. "Don't be so conventional. The rest may not be particularly interesting. Let's say that Eqbal is five foot eight and Marla is five foot nine. That could make them an inch more interesting than some couples. Even then, their height is not all that relevant. It might be if she were a midget, perhaps. Or a giant. Or if they were both dwarfs. Or had unusual physical traits. A wandering eye. Four toes. Even that might not mean much. How would four toes alter your person? Probably not at all. Your shoes might be handmade. But even that is optional, I believe.

"In this case, they are average in that regard. What isn't average is their seething. I would guess that most couples don't seethe. Though that's the kind of fact you can't ever deduce from taxes. I wonder if it would be possible to do a study, however, which showed that couples who gave five to ten percent of their money to a cause had better sex lives. That might be a wonderful incentive for a charity study. Perhaps I shall write a letter of proposal." He looked happy, maybe because she continued to smile.

The room took on a warmish quality as they continued their conversation. Arlette attempted to encourage Harbinger to proceed, although on his own he had plenty of ideas. Lesson one drew to a close. They both were pleased.

Jake called right after Harbinger left. They'd been back from their trip for a week. The trip had been good for them both. They felt closer to each other.

He rarely called in the middle of the day, and Arlette wondered if something was wrong that he didn't want to tell her. His voice sounded forced. His tone was muffled. How Jake felt was always mysterious. He wasn't one of those people who constantly feigned cheerfulness, but he didn't show anger either. His remoteness was often clearest in the topics he chose to discuss, as though his conversation was just an exercise.

"There's a show downtown I thought I'd suggest," he said, in a tone that implied that he was angry and hurt. "You may have other plans. Some people here liked it," he went on, without becoming any less muffled. "And although the topic is not something I have any great interest in, I thought we might consider going. I don't know why," he said.

Arlette knew him well enough to believe that nothing she could reply would satisfy him. "What is it? Will you tell me, or do you want me to say yes or no just like that? If that's the case, then yes, I'll come to the show."

"I don't like your placating me," he said. "Let me tell you first, and you can give me an honest answer." His voice got deeper the more upset he became, as though he were descending into darkness.

"The show is called *Animal Dreams*. It's about storybook animals, drawn or stuffed. Artists were asked to make animals for reasons having to do with ecology, nostalgia, or perversity. It might be worth seeing just for that. Did I ever tell you I loved my bear? I held on to him for years."

"What bear? Are you OK?" she asked. "Do you feel sick?"

"Why? Because I'm not completely rational and in control? Because I expressed love? Don't go overboard. It was only a bear. His name was Alexander Moon. Don't ask me why. I had a period where I called him Goo, but I went back to Moon. If anyone asked, I'd tell them the bear was Alexander. I kept my name for him a secret. He was brown, which I suppose is what they all are. With black button eyes. I slept with him long past the time when I was supposed to have lost him. Or grown up. I said he was somewhere in my room, but I kept him hidden in my airplane-equipment drawer. I liked the bear better."

"Is this a confession?" she asked. "Are you sure you're OK? You don't sound like yourself."

"Are you interested in my bear or not?" he asked. "At least tell me that."

"Of course," she said.

"Did you have one too?" he asked. "We have never discussed our childhood, really. Last week it came up for the first time. So briefly."

"I had a doll I loved. I forgot about her for years. She had a tea set, and she and I would have tea parties. She heard all my complaints about my relatives. I would report to her," she said.

"What was her name? What did she look like? How big was she? Were her lips very red?"

"I don't know that you've ever been this interested in me," she said, suddenly dubious. "In this particular way. Are you doing a festival on films of children and their pets? Or stuffed animals? Is there something behind this?"

"I'd like to know you better," he said.

"Through my childhood toys?"

Dear Arlette,

We met once at a conference of Jewish feminists
reevaluating our role in America. I remember
nothing of the conference, although I did save
your card, which says Book Doctor on it, in bold
letters (I guess you know that.) I want to write a
funny Haggadah. I need help. How I need help is
another question. I want it to be genuinely funny
and not, at best, merely cute, or at worst,
sophomoric. And also, I don't want it to be
interpreted as self-hating. I'm not.

Also, the book will not be a real Haggadah, but a
parody. Like *Snooze* parodies *The New Yorker*.

Here are some ideas:

1. Jokes about matzahs and, maybe, bitter herbs,
gefilte fish, and haroset. Haroset jokes might be
hard to find, though I'm confident I could write a
few. Matzah jokes should be easy enough. I'm sure
the great Jewish comics have told them. They might
be on some comic internet index.

2. Funny illustrations. Visual parting of the Red
Sea jokes. Cartoons. Moses and where he really
went. That kind of thing.

3. The story as told by famous authors, such as
Woody Allen, Toni Morrison, Alice Walker, Philip
Roth, Nadine Gordimer, and Grace Paley. As you can
see, the authors don't have to be Jewish. Maybe we
should include Norman Mailer, Bob Dylan, Ernest
Hemingway, Gertrude Stein, Maxine Hong Kingston,
and Alice Munro.

4. I'd like to play around with the Four Questions
part. Like Four Questions You'd Like to Ask Right
Now No Matter What (that may or may not be
relevant to the seder, such as: When in the world
will this end? Any four could be good here).

5. A section speculating on what might really have happened during the forty days and nights the Jews wandered through the desert. Orgies? Study groups? Book clubs? Dancing?

6. A kind of Seder Hall of Fame section, including information about the longest seder ever held, the biggest, the shortest, the most endless, etc.

7. A Pharaoh section, debunking the myth of Pharaoh's power. You know, kind of a *National Enquirer* "Who Pharaoh Really Was."

8. Politically correct multicultural feminist versions of the story, to be written by authors with an eye to humor. Here I'd suggest Cornel West and bell hooks, Sonia Sanchez, Barbara Ehrenreich, David Sedaris, and others.

9. New Passover Foods. Here we can go wild. We can ask Ben and Jerry for Passover flavors, for instance. Egyptian Date, Red Sea Cherry, Golden Calf Vanilla, Moses Melon.

10. Songs. Modern versions of some old favorites, like Dayenu and Had Gadya.

What do you think of this idea? I know you come across many books a day. Or a few, anyway. I don't really know how successful you are.

Would you like to participate in this? In what capacity? And what do you think my chances are for money? I heard you like Haggadahs. It's a thing, like cookbooks. I know that for a fact.

In spite of my sterling reputation, or maybe because of it, I am constantly broke. Could I make any money on this?

Yours, M

Dear M. I do like Haggadahs. And yours in
particular. You don't need me. You are all set to
go. Publish it yourself. A lot of Haggadah authors
do just that. I will buy one. Good luck with this.
It's a very good idea. AR

I I

taxes

Dear Arlette (I hope you don't mind my calling you that).

Harbinger sat at his desk most of the time, writing or not. It was a fitting steel gray. Clean and unassuming. A desk that looked like taxes.

I am inspired to write to you, he began. And then he stopped, and examined his office. It was neat, with places for all his objects. Even his paper clips had a box. He suddenly wished he had something there that was unexpected, something out of place. But what would it be? A Georgia O'Keefe painting, maybe. He had seen her calendar in the bookstore, and was particularly taken with her poppies. They'd seemed so red.

A big flower, with a scrawl in the corner, intimate and friendly: To Harbinger Singh, who saved me money. In admiration, Georgia. That would do. But she was dead. He'd read that somewhere. Maybe he could buy something, walk into a store and just buy an object that he wouldn't normally consider. Something impractical, yet alluding to his new life. But in a way which wasn't overly pointed. A copy of Proust, maybe. Although that might be too much. Too obvious and bookish, and intended to impress. A book wouldn't do. Maybe an Indian sculpture, small and brass, unobtrusive yet certain, of a couple frozen forever while making wild love. The man's genitals would be extensive, long, sharp, well polished. Extra-long. The woman would be both big breasted and enraptured. Together they'd look pleasured, frozen. He could make a small placard, even, a third of an index card: Marla and friend. He smiled.

He took out his tax pen and continued to write to her. He used his legal pad, always yellow, always neat. In order. I want to write to you. I don't know why. There is something about you that inspires me to write. I don't mean to imply that I find you inspirational, although you may well be. But we hardly know one another, and I'm not sure we ever will. Or will we? But I believe that you are the audience I've been looking for. That's different from saying that you are my audience. Probably not. I know this last is the writer's dilemma: how to find an audience. Everyone is looking. Even my tax clients. They want someone to hear their story. I listen, though not to everything. Only to what relates to my task.

Taxes can be large. I don't want to give you the wrong impression of my job, however. My love is computers. Have I told you that before? Maybe not. I hope this will emerge in my writing. I want to try to work it in. But I know enough to recognize that not all this will be present in the first novel. Maybe computers will be in the second. Or the third. I intend to write many. Legal murders, perhaps. The protagonist, a likable Indian tax lawyer, solves crimes in a graceful and humorous manner. I can see it now. Ben Kingsley as Harbinger Singh. I hope you aren't thinking to yourself, "just another prosaic author," or even worse, "another dollar in the bank." I would not like to be thought of in monetary terms. There's a certain irony there, I realize. Should this letter have a message? Perhaps. And should that message be greater than what I have already implied, that I am grateful for a reader? Should I make reference somehow to my Indianness? I sometimes believe that is what's expected of me. Should I talk about the Bhagavad Gita? Or mention the movies of Satyajit Ray? He is our master, you know. Not mine, especially, but ours in the larger sense. Indians like him, because he is prolific, and because he is able to show big worlds in short time periods. I read that once. Don't ask me where. It's not the kind of thing I'd remember. By the way, I thought of another detail for my heroine. I'd like *Anna Karenina* to be her favorite book. (Her actual favorite book was *One Minute Manager*. Does that matter? My sister Shaila loved *Anna Karenina*. She is a pediatrician in Seattle. Her husband is no Vronsky. Whose is?

His office seemed less gray. His next client, a stage manager who'd once been married to an actor in *La Cage aux Folles*, had serious tax problems, the kind Harbinger could solve. He knew she considered him a hero. He wondered if she was interested in him romantically. Maybe he would invite her to lunch. She had her charms.

I hope you won't think me presumptuous for writing this letter to you. What I'm presuming is only that you'll read it. It's up to me to make you do that, to engage you in the ways I know how. Writing is a kind of seduction, I know, but the reader is unknown, and so the task is harder than it might be otherwise. You don't know what kind of flowers to buy.

Your Harbinger Singh.

When Harbinger's letter arrived, Arlette had been home all day. She was working on a manuscript about gnostics, lost in the details of someone else's thoughts. At four, she walked down to the lobby to get her mail. When she saw his envelope, she felt surprisingly happy. She read his letter three times through before walking upstairs. She knew she should not write back to him. She wanted to be as professional as she could. But part of her wanted to respond, to keep a journal of her replies to Harbinger Singh. She would be entirely honest, say anything that occurred to her, knowing that he would never see what she wrote. She was a person who wrote many letters she did not mail. But she saved them, in folders, just in case.

Dear Harbinger, she began, writing in a red notebook that she'd saved for a while.

I'm glad you wrote to me. Not many people do. Strangers, of course, but not people I know a little better than that. There was a time a while ago when I wrote letters all the time. I wrote to everyone I met. I traveled then, and wrote long descriptions of what I saw to friends: villages, train rides, people I'd met. Once, outside of Athens, I was on a train that hit two women, and they died. I wrote a long letter describing the ride and their deaths to a friend named Emily. I haven't seen her in years, and in a way the letter about the women dying is more real to me than she is.

I stopped writing letters for a few reasons, I guess. I stopped being sure of what I wanted to say. Once I didn't have the easy material that being away provided, I really felt at a loss. I've never been very good at discussing my own life. And I'm not logical enough to pick a random subject and write about it in an interesting way. My attempts at this are wooden.

I've always loved letters. Receiving them especially. Even a handwritten envelope has a real satisfaction. And the promise that something personal or revealing, something written only for me, is inside. Maybe that's why I am a Book Doctor.

To get other letters, I have to write them, and that's been a problem. I say the reason is time: that I don't have time for more than a note, that I am busy with my work and my life, that I don't have the right pen, or the right kind of paper. Or the right period of time to do the proper job. But every day I read about other people and their books. People who write novel after novel, while riding to work on the subway, or in half-hour increments while taking care of four children. People like Joyce Carol Oates, who write books in their sleep, and when they're in the shower.

About your book, it is a beginning, not an end. The point is not the book but the writing. Once you are able to make writing a part of your life, and that isn't easy, your life will be changed. I don't mean in a big way necessarily. You won't get another job, or marry a different kind of woman, or walk to work down different streets. Your bedroom won't look different either, although it could. But once you let yourself begin to describe whatever you see, the process of seeing itself is altered. You have a way to put the pieces together, or pretend. The kind of writing you do doesn't matter. Neither does its future.

Dear Harbinger, I will probably never write you a real letter, for reasons having to do with my own inhibitions, I suppose. I am a very private person. I would not allow myself to

reveal very much. Except in this notebook. Where I will sort
of write to you.

To: Arlette Rosen
Editor at Large
The Fourth of July

Re: Matters Spiritual

I have assembled, after fifteen years, an
anthology, unique in its field, temporarily titled
Mysticism, Philosophical Analysis, and Words.
(I believe this is called a working title.) The
essays address a complex question: How does one
create a language, as well as a philosophy, about
an experience generally understood as ineffable?
Take this one example. A Zen koan is a linguistic
device whose purpose is to transcend language. How
can that be?

Some of the essays, all written by strenuous
religious and cultural experts, many of them
premier scholars in their fields, address critical
topics such as: Jewish mysticism and its very rich
texts; love language in Christian and Jewish
mysticism; Buddhist and Christian texts; and
Chan/Zen Buddhism. These essays are all informed
by a rigorous reading of the textual tradition.

This volume is not for the casual browser, but for
the serious scholar interested in mining these
works for their many insights into faith, belief,
language, and practice.

Here's where you come in. I need a reader, first of
all. Someone out of this highly specialized field.
Informed, but not so much so that one prejudice or
another will get in the way. And, too, there has
to be some kind of uniformity here, before we go
to the publisher.

My own CV is enclosed. I am currently director
emeritus of the Religious Consultation Center,
Diocese of Queens. I was the founder and
coordinator of the Guelph Center of Spirituality,
in Guelph, Ontario, where I ran many symposiums.
Perhaps that's enough. I am enclosing a stamped,
self-addressed envelope for your immediate reply.

Lawrence Gilles, SJ

12

love and marriage

"Harbinger, it's me. Carla." She sounded crisp and efficient, well informed. He knew she was sitting at a large, clean desk, freshly dusted. She dusted her desk first thing. Her habits were certain. He liked that. His too. He kept a feather duster in his lower left hand drawer.

It was eight in the morning. Both Harbinger and Carla had been at their jobs for an hour. She was an early riser. She woke up and exercised right away. She never hesitated, and used no excuses either.

Then she took her shower, made her coffee, and read through the headlines. He could see her right in front of him, neat and in place. All ready to go.

"Why, yes," he replied, hoping his voice sounded deep. Sometimes when he was nervous, his voice would escalate, traveling up the scale with embarrassing rapidity.

"Harbinger, is that you?" she said.

"Who else would it be? You know quite well that I am the only one on this line. If not me, then my voice mail. With which you are very familiar. 'This is Harbinger Singh. I'm unfortunately out at the moment with a client. You have two options. Either leave a message now if you like, or press pound for Donna who will record your information with paper and pen.' This is a truth you know well," he said.

"You seem to be in a peculiar mood. Would you like me to call back? I'm interested in a very straightforward conversation," she said, with uncharacteristic frankness. "I wanted to talk. Something came up with Dr. Stein yesterday that I felt I should discuss with you. Would you be more comfortable if we made a telephone appointment? Or if we waited for our dinner? Are you busy? Is a client on the way? Or right there? Please tell me, Harbinger. Just let me know."

"Why no," he said. "Not at all. I am as alone as one can be, in an office. There are other people here of course, but they are distanced by tasks and walls and preferences. It is early. A certain amount of leeway is associated with eight a.m."

"Harbinger," she repeated. "Are you really OK? Would you like me to come over? Do you feel well? You don't seem like yourself. You sound odd. It's true that you are an unusual person, but not this much." He didn't answer right away. There was silence between them.

"*Weird* is more the word," he said. "I sound weird. Perhaps I am far too unaccustomed to expressing my personality. What you have heard, all these years, is merely a kind of camouflage. Necessary demeanor. My formula for person-hood. A disguise in place of actual Singh. A person who was-n't. A man who could not be. An Indian who was actually Egyptian. A Copt disguised as a Sikh. And you, Carla Weiland, are actually a torch singer of welfare rights, an impassioned public champion of heart-wrenching ballads. The kind that Elvis the Pelvis made famous."

"Harbinger, please stop. I am truly worried now," she replied. "I can tell something is wrong. All right, so I won't bring up my therapy conversation. It can wait. That can't be what this is about. You sound like a different person. Has something changed? Are you having an affair? Is that what this is?"

"An affair?" he shouted into the phone. "What differ-ence could that possibly make to you? You told me a year ago that we were free to lead our separate lives. That I could go. Run wild if I preferred. Exercise my baser animal urges. Those were your words exactly. I've written them down, so that I could remember just what you said. Whatever I did was of no concern to you. Unquote. We were platonic friends. We would always be friends. Nothing had changed between us. Except that we would now live apart. That's all, you said. That's all. I was now, according to your formulation, de-sexed, but not entirely. My urges were to be directed elsewhere, and we could still continue our conversation at dinner. As I understand it, that was your idea. Correct me if I've gotten this wrong, because it's very possible that your overly clear language was in fact surreptitious."

"Harbinger," Carla said, eking out the syllables very slowly, "you knew it was over as well as I did. That there was no point. Neither one of us wanted to stay together. It wasn't just my idea. In fact, you were the one who began the process of our separation. If you remember. And I thought we both agreed that we are happier now. Wasn't that a conclusion we reached at one of our dinners?"

"Happier?" he shouted into the phone, so loudly that one of the secretaries from down the hall ran rapidly into his office, unaccustomed, perhaps, to hearing the word *happy* from Harbinger, loudly or not.

"Mr. Singh?" said Gloria tentatively. She was all in pink. She leaned into his room very cautiously.

"One minute, if you please," he smiled at her. He did not cover the phone. "I am expressing a kind of happiness, in an unusual way. Do forgive me." To Carla, he continued his harangue.

"Do I want you back?" His voice erupted a little too loudly. "Why of course not. No I don't. Not at all. But does that make any of this any easier? No again to that," he said. "No again. However if you would like to discuss this in a more rational way, I suggest we continue at our weekly dinner. Our meal. When we come together for several hours, to reaffirm our bond."

"Harbinger, I wonder if you should consider tranquilizers," Carla said nervously. "Do you feel depressed? I can ask Doctor Stein, if you like."

"How condescending of you," he replied. And then, "Farewell, my Carla. As abrupt as this might seem. I'm off to the quietly exciting world of taxes. A world that knows neither race nor creed. Goodbye," he said, and hung up.

Later, in his notebooks, he made her writhe uncomfortably.

She wanted him, his Marla. That he knew. There was no stopping her desire. It was boundless, unfettered. Maybe even unquenchable. The more he gave, the more she wanted. On occasion, Eqbal, for reasons he never revealed, would disappear. He would vanish somewhere, to a mistress, maybe, or a second apartment he'd privately maintained for years. He'd have a second, different life. Maybe there'd even be children. Marla never knew where, and she didn't dare to ask. She'd do anything to keep him living with her.

A Visit to Arlette Rosen's Apartment
by Harbinger Singh

(We did not decide how long these descriptions should be. This first will be short. Just to give me an idea of the exercise itself. I have actually done very little, in the way of practice exercises. What I've done in my professional life has mostly consisted of tax law. As you know. I've done many practice taxes, however. Like this: If Vance earned $100,000 one year for his work as an interior designer, and the following year he did four lobbies but was stiffed for his fees and lost $50,000, should we carry the loss backward or forward?)

It was nearly 8:15 by the time I left my small, neat, climate-controlled apartment, my anonymous, air-conditioned box which I, for reasons of lost love, now call home. I was apprehensive. About the same as I am when I have to face a moderately difficult audit. In an audit, the outcome is often very much tied to the chemistry between auditor and client. It's much like a trial. Some clients do a better job defending themselves than I do. They just click with the auditor, in a very lucky way. Sometimes, though, the auditor and I, accustomed to speaking a language which masks as a disinterested set of numbers, have a certain rapport. It's a little like playing a good tennis game between partners who each know the rules. When the teams are equal, the games are more satisfying.

At Arlette's, I feel I don't know the odds. It is difficult to read her attitude toward me. At first, she seemed both condescending and distant, a little superior, as though she understands something about sentences that I can never grasp. What could that be? Is she right, or is she wrong? I think she likes me better now.

She's not entirely sympathetic to my plan for The Revenge. On the other hand, she's often receptive. But cautiously so. She doesn't seem respectful of the idea of writing a best seller. Why would that be? I know it isn't easy. Stephen King is a man of many talents. And I don't pretend to be a William Shakespeare, also a best-selling author, I believe. One of the biggest. I'm doing this for reasons other than enlightenment, or money. I know about the range of reasons. I hear them every day. How people spend their money is an occasion for much creative speculation. The reasons they give are the way I come to know them.

As for Arlette (her? you?), she seems mysterious, attractive, a little bit distant. A very different bird.

Her apartment is small. It's crowded with things. Books. (I don't know what else is there. I'll have to look again.) She isn't small herself.

Is that enough? It's hard to do this. I see things, but I don't usually describe them. If I could create a column of numbers to ascribe to you, I suppose I'd do a better job. But then, I would not be stepping off into the unknown. One of those numbers, by the way, would be lucky eleven.

I tried. Keep that in mind.

Once again, she took out her red notebook. She'd write him back, and he'd never know. How funny that someone like Harbinger Singh made her feel like writing.

Here is my version. (Yours was fine. The point is to see that this can be done in many different ways. I'm sure you know that.)

It was a very hot day. So hot, you felt as if you were breathing the same damp wet air over and over and over again. It was hard to feel anything but tired. I poured a glass of ice water, and then could barely drink it. I squeezed a lemon into the water for something to do.

When I heard the doorbell, I felt more exhausted than anything else. Another writer. Another book. Sometimes I wish I could ban this sentence: I have a (good, great, unique, money-making, best-selling) book idea.

When I first saw Harbinger Singh, I wasn't sure what his book would be like. Writers sometimes look like their books. Scrupulous neat older women write mysteries like they are: all in good order, with characters named Maud or William or Claire. But their books can be very bloody.

Harbinger Singh looked like no book I know. He talked about revenge, but in a way that had nothing to do with murder. He seemed to want his book to be a nation-state of Singh, complete with a theme song. And maybe even a flag, a bird, or a flower. I've never met an author with those aspirations. The idea of writing a best seller, though, is far too familiar. Lawyers seem especially prone. They all think their cases, even if they're wills and estates, are fascinating subjects. To me, reading briefs is like watching paint dry. I reserve judgment still on Harbinger Singh. (On you, Mr. Babu.)

At our first meeting, he was nervous and overly polite. But then he wrote, and returned a second time, and seemed to be serious enough to want to continue. Some people like the idea of writing a book more than they like the actual process of writing: long hours alone, hours when even the simplest words won't come. This is true, by the way, no matter what the subject. But hard does not seem to be the problem for Harbinger. Or is it? I will stop here, for various reasons.

Arlette Sophia Rosen, sans degree

13

untevye

It was still too hot. Nothing moved. The day was stuck inside itself, and even the flies circled in slow motion, moving through sludgy brown air. Cold was a memory, remote and unfamiliar. When Jake called to suggest a movie, the only reasonable option short of a shower, Arlette could only say yes. Movies—no matter how dense or slow, no matter the subject—movies were always air-conditioned. Walt Disney or Jean-Luc Godard, in the summer they were the same, dark and cool.

Arlette often believed that most of her relationships were spent in the dark, not at home, but in the movies, in those rooms where intimacy was something that happened to other people on a screen, and audiences watched. She thought about this often, thought how much both she and Jake wanted to be characters in a Fellini film, not only Marcello and Juliette. Even extras, people milling around in one of those beautiful Italian towns, swaying through their lives to Nina Rota music. Instead they were locked in to something else altogether, to a kind of remove that often seemed wrong.

Almost out of nowhere, Arlette wanted something else: a child, a dog, a loud messiness, the messiness of real life, a life she didn't have.

"Would you like to come downtown to the Kurosawa?" said Jake. "I'm sure you'll like it. It's an old movie about homeless people who live in a world of magical realism. It's called *Do Do Kan*. But if you're not in the mood, there's a new Clint Eastwood. And an old documentary about Malcolm X." He sounded gentle, even comforting. "If you're in a more esoteric mood," he continued, "there's *L'Age D'Or*, an old Buñuel, before *Un Chien Andalou,* that he wrote with Salvador Dalí. It was scandalous when it appeared," he said, "and if you haven't seen it, it's a classic of its kind."

"No classics," she replied. "Only air-conditioning. The specifics don't matter. But I don't want to think. I just want to watch. If that's possible. I know that's not your first choice," she said. "But I can hardly move today."

"Why don't you buy an air-conditioner?" he asked. "I don't think they're all that expensive. Or a fan, at least. Some small window fan. I can help you. I've seen them everywhere."

"You don't have one either," she said, petulantly.

"Maybe we'll buy two," he replied, in a good-natured tone. "Matching fans. Black and white. Though that wouldn't really be matching, would it?"

"I don't want Buñuel," she said. "Anything else. But nothing disturbing in that particular way. And I want popcorn. Not flavored."

"You know I don't like flavored either," Jake added.

"I want fake liquid butter, very bright yellow, with a lot of salt. Did I ever tell you about the time I went to the movies when I was a child? Popcorn toppings were free. Do you remember? I stood in back of the fattest person I'd ever seen. She was enormous. She had blonde hair tied back with a bright orange ribbon into a big ponytail. Everyone was watching her. And she talked loudly enough so we didn't have to strain. She said to the man behind the counter, 'Do you know all the people who come to the counter and ask you to leave off their butter? Well I'll take all of theirs.'

"Now your turn," she said. "It doesn't have to be popcorn related."

"I'll see what I can do," he said. "Can it be from public radio?"

"Source doesn't matter."

"Well I heard this a few days ago. They had their story-telling festival, although this isn't a legitimate story. It was told by a woman from Ireland. Her name was Barbara, but the announcer made it a point to spell it out, so we'd see it wasn't the usual Barbara. It's spelled b-a-i-r-b-r-e. She's a teacher of Gaelic from County Clare. She is the only girl, in a family of nine brothers.

"They all hated church, so every Sunday morning, they'd pretend to go to church, but instead they'd walk to the pub down the block, and listen to the conversation, until it was time to go home for Sunday lunch. A man named Jack was their hero in the bar. Jack was a very big drinker. One Sunday she and her brothers were sitting at a big table by the door. Jack got up to leave, and as the door opened, they saw the priest from church walk by. His name was Father Peter. No one liked Father Peter. He was very pompous. They all heard him say, 'Drinking again, Jack.' 'Me too, Father,' Jack replied."

They laughed together. A few seconds later, Arlette spoke very softly. "Do you love me?"

"What is this, *Fiddler on the Roof*?" he answered, though not unkindly.

"I want to know."

"Can this wait until we are together? Is it something you have to know now?"

"No. Yes."

"Can I show you later? Then my answer won't just be an idea. Easy words."

"Tell me now. And tell me later again."

"I love you," he said. "I love you again. Is that clear enough? I can say it in other ways, if you like. I really do love you, Arlette."

"Thank God for that," she replied. "I love you, too. But you know that."

"What makes you so sure I know?"

They both liked the movie, the Kurosawa, and by the time they left the heat had faded a little. In the café next door, Arlette read to Jake.

```
Dear Arlette,

How are you?

I have in my possession a novel chronicling the
rise and fall of a love affair. A friend of ours
(yours and mine) wrote this with her lover. She
doesn't want me to tell you her name. (I don't
know who he is.) He and she wrote alternating
chapters. They each describe, from their own
perspective, the details of their affair.

Boaz and Ruth is a modern love story. They are
each married to other people. They are happy
enough in their marriages. But they manage to fall
```

together one April day. They chronicle the path of
their affair, and how it affects other parts of
their lives.

It's a Volvo novel. Kids in the car, small
leitmotifs of passion. The characters order their
clothing in the mail, and only wear solid colors
made from natural fabrics. They drink wine and go
to Deer Isle, or Wellfleet. You know them, I'm
sure. They are cautious and familiar, always in
control.

They are very attracted to one another. Sex plays
a big part in this book. They have sex all the
time. In the car, for instance. Also, on table
tops and desks, in pay-phone booths, and on big
gray rocks. In Central Park near the reservoir,
and in the Statue of Liberty torch. These scenes
are well described, and comprise 80 percent of the
novel. The other 20 percent breaks down as
follows: 10 percent how they met and began their
relationship. Another 10 percent on the
(inevitable) end of their affair.

As it stands, the story has a little too many
details, and they don't know themselves what to
cut out. I said I would be their John Alden, and
ask you to help. Will you?

Elizabeth "Mimi"
Williams

"What do you think?" she asked. Jake hadn't said a word.

"Another Yuppie redemption novel," he said. "The world
is their sex life, more or less. It's all about gratification, of
one kind or another. Have you noticed how much food there
is in those novels? Chanterelle mushrooms and two-hundred-
dollar bottles of wine?"

"Is that all so bad? What's wrong with eating well? We try, don't we? Besides you don't hate it in Cheever novels. Or do you?"

They did not go home together. They each wanted to be in their own apartment. At home, hot and tired, she wrote in her journal.

I find it very hard to talk to Jake directly. The truth is, I lead all of my life in a very indirect manner. I don't know why that is. Could that be what my book obsession is about? A kind of voyeurism, a way of living my life indirectly? Maybe we're both like that. Films, after all, are as voyeuristic as they come. My sessions with Harbinger Singh have thrown me off. There he is, right in the middle of his life without a scrim to separate him from the rest. I am not romanticizing who he is. And I'm not in love with him either. He clearly isn't my type. Why is that, I wonder? We are all so limited in the ways we can see. So boxed in by what's expected and by ideas of appropriateness. I am sorry for all that in myself. I wish it were otherwise.

14

tv movies

It was time for Harbinger's usual Wednesday appointment. Arlette was more nervous than usual. Was she becoming too friendly with this man? Her other clients and their books seemed more remote. Certainly very separate from her life. Although she was addicted to them, they didn't intrude. With Harbinger, it was something else. She often found herself preoccupied with his life. Who was he, after all?

She rarely thought about writers in that way. What they wanted was nearly always simple: to tell their story, or a story they knew, in a way that would bring them fame and even money. To have a TV movie made from their book, and then to appear on Jay Leno, explaining how they did it. To be acknowledged for the story they really wanted to tell. And finally did, with great success because at last, everyone listened.

Arlette liked Harbinger, and she didn't. Why did he marry Carla to begin with? Why was he still in love? Was it real? Was it an idea he had of who she might have been? Why would someone like Harbinger want to write a book? She didn't believe his book could be any good. But what did that matter?

She dressed carefully, as though he were about to pay attention to all the details she'd chosen: all loose, all white. She wondered if white were an Indian symbol. Perhaps she would seem to be a pure and holy cow, a sacred, untouchable object. The idea made her smile.

She straightened the room for Harbinger Singh, intending to understand him, and what he wanted. But when she heard Harbinger at the door, pounding and shouting, "It's Babu right here," in a friendly, insistent way, she lost her usual sense of distance, and just opened the door very simply, leading him down her hall to the couch.

"Haldora," he smiled at her, "You are now Haldora," he repeated. "That's quite a name, I must say. Babu has nothing on Haldora. It's Scandinavian, by the way. Norwegian, in fact. I heard it once. It belonged to a very beautiful clothing designer. Her clothes had a quiet elegance. Sounds like a restaurant. I'll bet you thought I didn't know anything like that. That I didn't even notice. Untrue. I know much more than seems evident at first. Part of the reason is my clients. They are diverse, and they tell me things. Doing taxes is a little like being an analyst of some kind. You listen to secrets all the time.

"I wanted to propose to you that perhaps our names can vary, week to week. That we don't keep our roles quite as fixed as either of us are accustomed to. That I sometimes be the doctor and you the client. Or is it patient? I'm sure you're thinking to yourself, 'Then who will pay the bill?' Well, I certainly will, I guarantee. It is your terrain, after all.

"Even I know that the idea of your paying me would be very foolish. Unless of course you were doing your taxes. But even there," he paused, "even there, I would like to make room for what might develop. If, for example, you came to me with the idea that you yourself would be willing and able to do them on your own, and yet you had a need, for who knows what reason, to sit in my chair, to use tools, my computer, my tables, my current information, my modern facilities for doing your taxes with ease, you'd be my guest. In that case however, the payment would be all yours. We'd be on my turf, as this is yours."

Arlette watched carefully as he paused for a minute just to breathe, and then began again.

"As I was saying," he continued, "if this is truly to be a full creative exercise, then let it be that. If I am to execute my revenge for Carla's lackluster attitude toward my entire being, more or less, then I must play around with possible forms of expression. And while I am reluctant to admit this to you, this forum, this small room in an apartment I do not know very well, is more or less my only opportunity for that to happen. Let the music play," he shouted, "Haldora or whoever you are today." And then he added, with his more customary formality, "Maybe you have some thoughts on all this. Or on me. Please," he said. "Be honest. It could be of use to us both."

"Haldora may have been a mistake," she replied gravely. "I'm not sure it suits me. I am not quietly elegant. But I'm not an Arlette either."

"Well, one name should not have to contain any one of us," he said. "Sometimes when I am sitting in my chair at work, my familiar brown accountant's chair, nicely leather, a chair where I have spent most of my days as a working professional, I think to myself, 'I can't possibly be Harbinger Singh, LLD, CPA.' There's no way. I must be someone else, someone with a voice that is more basso profundo. I would like to be more Italian, perhaps, more Pavarottiesque. I would like to boom forth melodically, rather than speak with the deferential mumble that seems to accompany my profession. I'd like to smoke Marlboros, drive a Jaguar, and write a book about a case I won, a fascinating litigation involving every kind of spy and love incident, with global implications and a captivating trial, a trial that keeps the international jury sequestered for many weeks. Here I am instead, a simple Sikh tax lawyer from Queens with an interest in computers, seeking revenge on my one and only ex-wife Carla by putting her into a tightly spangled bright red dress, more or less. How about Ved?" he added, as an afterthought. "Does that suit me?" And then he sat down, light sweat on his brow, half-smiling.

"Please take notice," he continued, looking Arlette right straight in the center of her eyes, "I am ready for a creation that's as much imagined as real."

Arlette swallowed. She didn't know what else to say, so she hummed very briefly. Hoping that this would be his answer. She hummed "Frere Jacques" in Hebrew. A camp song called "Hinei MaTov." She remembered it very suddenly.

"Good, good," he nodded. "It's always good to hum."

"Today," she said, "we'll work on writing spontaneously. I will give you the first sentence, and you can continue from there."

"Can I pick my own first sentence?"

"O.K. But what will that first sentence be?"

"How about *I wish it all were otherwise*? Didn't you say that before? It's good," he enthused. "It has potential, I think."

"What might that be?"

"That's the story," he said. And then he began to write. And she did, too. In her red book which was beginning to be full.

Before Harbinger left, she asked, "What do you think of John Sayles?"

"Is he a client?" he asked. "Please remind me. Or is he an important American? I don't know them all offhand, just like that. But if you tell me something about him, I might know more."

"He's a writer and a filmmaker who made a lot of movies. He is politically correct. The class struggle, for instance, is often a part of his films."

"You mean he makes movies about people of color? One this, one that. The American potpourri. It's a nice idea. But what about Sikhs? Are they well represented in his films?" And then he laughed. "That would be something," he said. "I read in a local Indian newspaper—and there are many—that they were considering a Sikh doctor for *Chicago Hope*. Could that be true? They'd have to fly in Ben Kingsley." He laughed again.

"Goodbye, Ved." She walked him to the door, and they shook hands.

"Goodbye, good doctor." And then, he seemed to vanish.

And as soon as he left, she instantly felt his absence. She missed him.

At least she had her letters.

Mid-July, as the sun moves

Ms. Arlette,

What do you know about your soul? How intimate are you with your own inner universe, that infinite, mysterious, powerful space where your actual being is cracked wide open? When you peel away the rest of yourself, what's left is your soul. (Soul, by the way, implies that faith is a verb.)

I've written a book, simply titled *Your Soul Your Seed Your Garden,* which covers many subjects of self, and shows you, with clarity, how to navigate the deepest, richest paths of your own life. Drawing on the Renaissance, where people used the soul to transform their very beings, my book, *Your Soul Your Seed Your Garden,* covers these problems, and contributes solutions. There are actual answers in my book to these:

1. Loneliness. This is a universal problem, which ancient images can quickly resolve.

2. How to see your life as an ongoing art, with the soul as an artist in the center.

3. Negative thoughts. (I don't believe that the futile act of trying to stop them solves anything much.)

4. Your job, and what to do if it gets in the way of your soul. (Also, how to tell if that's the case.)

5. Eroticism, the soul, and your life. (How to have good sex and still be a spiritual person, in other words.)

Additionally, the book contains many great ideas from history, including thoughts and quotations from Plato, Blake, Hung, van Gogh and many, many more.

Does this interest you at all? You can be honest. Honesty is nearly as important to me as my soul.

I was a seminarian, a teacher, and a scholar, and now I am a full-time writer. I intend to write *Soul* Part II, when this is done. It's a little

harder going than I expected, though, and I need a
little help. Are you intrigued enough to say yes?
Arthur Duff

Dear Arthur Duff,

I'm not sure about the Soul. By that, I am not
referring to your book, which seems like a good
enough idea, I guess. I mean the Soul itself. What
is it? Will your book make it better? Stronger?
Easier to see or to feel? I don't know enough
about souls, my own or anyone else's, to really
help you. I would recommend your working with a
Jesuit book doctor, or a former Catholic priest,
or a seminarian. I know one, in fact. He is a
wonderful editor and an agonized soul himself,
fully engaged in the problems you explain. His
head is often in his hands. He drinks white wine,
chain smokes, and reads Viktor Frankl's *Man's
Search for Ultimate Meaning* on a regular basis.
Especially Greeks. He is in an agonizing study
group. I've recommended him to others in the past.
He's helped me more than once. His name is
Thaddeus G. J. Hoyt. (He is not a Ted.) You can
write to him directly at 41 West 83rd Street, New
York, New York 10024. He will be glad enough to
hear from you. But it will take him a while to
respond. He is very, very careful. In the end,
that will be of enormous help to you, in writing
your careful book.

Yours,

Arlette Rosen

Dear Arlette Rosenberg,

I have in my hands a rare collection of letters
that have been authenticated by several prominent

scholars. They are letters from Vanessa Bell to her cousin Alice, a midwife, farmhand, and baker of pies. I propose that these letters would be a wonderful book, of interest to many, many readers everywhere.

As you know, Vanessa Bell was in good company. A sister to Virginia, she was the center of the famous Bloomsbury group, people whose names I need not mention to someone in the book field like yourself, but will, just for the record: Leonard Woolf, Lytton Strachey, John Maynard Keynes, Roger Fry, Duncan Grant, and Ottoline Morrell. She talks about all of these people in her casual, unsentimental, sexually liberated way in her letters to cousin Alice, who frequently sends her seasonal recipes mostly for pickles and pies, with an occasional cake or two. I've tested them just to make sure. She includes a wonderful recipe for strawberry rhubarb in a butter crust. Their correspondence was very unique. I envision this book as *Cooking, Letters, and Life*.

As you know, too, I'm sure, Bell was a painter and decorative artist. She describes her work in some detail to Alice. Altogether there are 640 letters. Exactly half were written by Alice. Theirs seemed to be a perfectly egalitarian relationship, in spite of their obvious differences.

Assuming that one-third of them are interesting (one-third seems to be the average, wouldn't you say?) I believe there's enough here to make a fascinating book which would shed light on Bloomsbury itself, as well as on the well-loved Vanessa, a woman whose life was certainly complicated, as we all know. And her cousin Alice, who we only knew of slightly, until now.

I would like to edit these letters. It could help me with my tenure problem. Alice's niece Elizabeth

sent them to me in three shoe boxes because she
heard me deliver a paper a few years ago in
England on Bloomsbury: "What's Missing From Our
Records." She thought these letters might add a
piece to the puzzle. I believe she's right.

I have never edited letters before, and I need
some help, a consultation, perhaps, in knowing how
to do it. How can I tell what's interesting and
relevant? What are the rules for order? Is
chronology the only format? Or are there other
constraints?

I know you will help.

Yours,

Edna Kert

Dear Edna Kert,

What's interesting is instinctual. I might like a
letter you wouldn't. The letters sound as though
they have a lot of potential. You need an academic
to help you. Not me. I do love Vanessa Bell,
however. And wish you luck. Yours, AR

15

your tight abs

Carla and Harbinger had arranged to have dinner, not at their usual Bill's, but somewhere else. Harbinger suggested Gus's downtown and Carla quickly agreed. Gus's was almost festive. The restaurant, owned by an ageless and handsome Greek man who danced, sang, and constantly drank ouzo, had the carefree feeling of a fishing village. The posters were of cheerful sailing ships, of ruins that could have been nearly anywhere, happy villagers in festive markets, Rhodes and Crete and Samos.

Gus himself liked Greek music, old Theodorakis cassettes he played very loudly from a tape deck in the corner bar, where he stood, most nights, with a good-looking woman named Marie. They surveyed the guests with an unobtrusive watchfulness, making sure that mood and food were more than pleasant.

Harbinger heard about Gus's from Darlene at work, a red-haired woman who seemed happier than the others in his office. She would bounce in and out of Harbinger's office to say hello, and she'd often stand for a minute or two in his doorway, mentioning what she'd done the night before. She seemed to go out endlessly, to movies and plays and restaurants and music. She would mention her companions' names, Tom or William or Raoul or Ahmed, and although he never had the slightest idea who the men were who took her here and there, he enjoyed hearing Darlene's descriptions of what seemed like constant pleasure. She'd been very happy at Gus's.

Carla didn't protest. She willingly agreed to meet him at Gus's at seven, by the bar. When he arrived, she was already waiting. Although it was a very warm night, Carla looked cool. He supposed the word for her was *self-possessed*. Carla had an equanimity, a can-do-everything quality that Harbinger had always admired. She looked like a Paula, efficient and calm. They met in front of the restaurant, on a busy intersection, a constant festival of visitors from Tokyo, Hoboken, St. Paul, joining the Village parade.

On their first date, a night that seemed so many years ago, he had asked her what her aspirations were, and what impressed him so much at the time was that she answered his questions by producing a small black leather notebook trimmed in gold, which had as its first page a carefully composed list, numbered one through nine. Carla had nine aspirations. He didn't remember what they were now, but they'd all been high-minded.

Can that change? he had asked. Could your aspirations one day be three or eight or even forty-five?

Why no, she'd said very coolly. I've thought about these all my life. This is it. My agenda. A personalized program for me to lead a worthwhile life. And you? She asked. What are yours?

I am equally organized, he replied, in other ways. But not in that particular area of my life. I have some routines. I exercise, more or less on a daily basis. I jog, and walk, and do a reasonable amount of yoga. It's in my blood, he'd smiled. The way Jane Fonda is in yours. My sun salute is your tight abs.

She'd smiled back at him, but insisted he continue. My life plans are vague, he'd said. Some day we will be able to do anything we want, more or less, on a machine. And I intend to use that possibility to full advantage. To lead a productive life with a computer as my guide. It will be a phenomenal tool. It will free us of some of the problems of modern life. We can't yet know which ones.

And of course, I will always do taxes. Taxes are a measure, a form of keeping us grounded. But they are also irrelevant, in some way or other. Still with taxes we can tell a certain amount about a person, information that may be useful later. If I write a novel, perhaps, or a play, this kind of financial allocation may be useful in helping me make characters seem real.

Later, he remembered saying to Carla, in an odd moment between them, "I love you and I want to do your taxes." But she didn't smile, and answered no too quickly. "You'd know too much about details I have no desire to reveal."

That night at Gus's, the room seemed full of happy people, very ready to enjoy whatever they could. The air turned the lightest possible yellow, people in it nearly spinning with the kind of early-evening buoyancy that seems to appear in city summers, different from grasses and children and barbecues, a big-city lightness that just lifts everyone up with it and then changes the dimensions of the most familiar rooms. There were sounds of music, distant enough to appear more remembered than real, more a whisper than a call to dance. Then, too, there was the clatter of a good meal, effortless, restaurant-served, big white bowls of avolemono soup with thin perfect slices of lemons floating across the top, generous appetizers of smoky babaganoush, of pink salty tarama, of shiny black olives and vine leaves gently rolled. All this was part of the room, a room with no clear dimensions, with no shadows or hints of darkness. A room where everything said was in the best possible light, in the glow of Mediterranean kindness.

"Carla, have we ever really talked?" Harbinger began. "I don't know what we've said to one another all these years, or how. Why we came together in the first place, and then why we decided to fall apart."

"Yes and No and Yes," she said, but she didn't seem to really want to say much more about her life. Or even his. And so they spent their evening together, immersed in the usual unsatisfying banter of politics and issues, of near-ideas and controversies, in spite of the golden room.

That night, home alone in his small, neat apartment, secure and clean, with a cold bottle of water in his refrigerator and extra soap sitting where it belonged on the shower shelf, Harbinger began to work. For most of the night he stayed awake, forcing his hot-blooded Marla to scream out in desire, more than once. "I want it," she yelled. "And only you can give it to me. You're the only man I've ever met to satisfy my deep desires." He made her seethe and shout.

Before he finally went to sleep, he decided to replace *deep* with *raging*. He drew a thin, perfectly straight line through *deep,* and went to bed, satisfied.

Dear Arlette Rosen,

Annie Sequins gave me your name. I'm sure you've
heard of her. And she's heard of you. She's Jewish.
Most people don't know that.

I want to write a book entitled *How to Make Love
to a Man, a Woman, or Anything Else!* It could
change any reader's life. Besides providing
lovemaking information, techniques, historical
facts, and relevant literary examples, this book
could alter our love-possibilities. No longer would
we be sitting at home waiting for the Correct
Object for Lovemaking Purposes. Our fantasies would
not be restricted to ideas we already know. But we
would be able, by using the many tips here, to Make
Love With Anyone and Anything.

As you must know, I've written other lovemaking
books before, and they've always been successful.
My husband jokes that I could write *How to Make
Love to a Camel* and satisfy my readers. I wrote
them with a silent (but well-paid) collaborator.
She was the writer, actually. The ideas were mine.
She moved to Portland, Oregon, to pursue other
interests. So I'm looking for someone to take her
place.

We can meet, if you like. That might be a useful
way of airing concerns.

Yours,

Alexandra Dime

Alexandra,

No thanks. I'm not the one. Though maybe I should
be.

AR

16

a chainsmoking czech, just yvette

Another Appointment
by Harbinger Singh

I went to my fourth session of practice prose-writing with Haldora, my doctor, although MD are not the right initials and neither are BD. She might be more appropriately called Yvette. At least today. Yvette of darkening eyes. Arlette's eyes are not dark, but they could be. The eyes of a Haldora might be navy blue. I can see my horizons expanding. I might combine all of my impulses to write a megabook, a book about passionate sex, courtroom drama, family abuse, taxes, computers, and Lutretia, a woman in my office whose looks I've always admired. I think she has her MBA.

Arlette/Haldora/Yvette keeps telling me to keep my ambitions small. Write what you know, she says. Don't try Peter Matthiessen unless you've seen the Everglades. I wrote down that sentence, thinking it had the ring of truth to it. Who is Peter Matthiessen anyway? Someone must know. I'll ask around. I didn't dare to ask Yvette. She said it in such a definite way, as though he were a household word. Not my household. But I can't tell her that. She'd think I was not well read.

At least I know where the Everglades are. I told her I would like to write a novel of inescapable moral anguish. It looked to me like she was smirking. Moral Anguish, she said. All men want to write those novels. And then she recommended I try reading Graham Greene. Maybe I will. And maybe not. Do I want to be influenced? That's a pretty tough call. Of course I do, but not so much that the influence intrudes in any way.

So where are we now, my Yvette and me? First of all, she would probably say that she's not my Yvette. Of that I am almost certain. And then, there's another question in all this. Does she only want my money? Is hers a job like any other? Or are books a kind of religion? Not that it's money, exactly. It's time.

Does she want for me to write a good book so that she can have another successful client? *Thin Forever* is hers, I know.

And who truly knows if *Marla Up At The Bench* (or whatever) will actually get written? This could all be a frivolous exercise. It is my intention, of course, but I have had other intentions that I have not fulfilled. Like flying a plane. One difference here is that I am not actually paying a flight instructor. And I know that payment is linked in my own mind to seriousness.

Does Arlette pay taxes? That's occurred to me more than once, but the truth is, I don't much care.

So last week we sat in her room and did lawyer exercises. She was the client, I was the lawyer, and then we switched. For a while, we were both judges. Then we were both adversaries. We wrote down dialogues, and talked about courtroom drama. She likes them, and so do I.

I left satisfied that I was getting somewhere. Even if it's just somewhere else.

That night Arlette took out the red notebook again.

I have started thinking of names more intensely since you made the suggestion that we vary them. I must say I have never been very imaginative with my characters' names. For no good reason. Although I know how important names are. I will strike out all Susans and Dianes, all Carols and Lindas and Roberts. Once I wrote a short story about Lindas and Roberts all meeting together in a small town in Kansas, for a conference: the National Linda and Robert Weekend. The idea was that all Roberts and Lindas would meet, and discuss how their names affected who they became. What lives they lived. In my story, some Roberts and Lindas fell in love. It was up to the reader to match them together.

I'll try Emile, and Cicely (should I spell it Sisely?) and maybe Rif. Though Rif seems too far-fetched, too macho and Montana for me to know him well. Maybe Izzy. Someone told me yesterday about a girl named Elizabeth who calls herself Izzy. She could be a heroine.

If I were to choose a name for myself, it would be less "t" sounding than Arlette. Arlette feels like too many t's. Don't ask me why. I can't explain. I prefer open names, names without y's. (Yvette is a problem on both these counts.) Maybe Alma, or Cleo, or Havanna, or Syl.

Tex Taxes is funny, but not nearly as evocative, as perfect as Harbinger Singh. It will be hard for you to match that, I think. Very hard. Is Babu short for Babaloo, by the way? Or does it stand on its own? It reminds me of elephants, and tall men in jungles. I don't know how lawyerly it seems. Babu is more for the wilds than the courts.

About our last meeting, your theme songs seem like interesting choices, and I wonder once more if theater might not be a better place for your talents. You seem to enjoy the dramatic elements of writing: the voices, atmosphere, acting the part of all the characters. (I am more the kind of person who sits in a chair, looks out the window, and writes a word or two. I could never tell you the theme song for my novel, for example. How it sounds is a question I can't begin to answer. I don't know what it should smell like either. Here too, I'd probably stay with mossy. Fir trees.)

I am changing a little in my attitude toward you, and even in my work. Though how, I can't say. It's a feeling, very subtle and unfamiliar. But there, I am sure. Just how, I have to see.

Here is my official summary, for you.

To continue the story, Harbinger Babu knocked on my door, and I was very glad to see him. He is full of wonderful ideas. He is inspired, and alive, in ways I've rarely seen. Some days I think I should be paying him. He is the most creative person I have ever met. He is causing me to reconsider him and everything else. Even my own life.

Time disappears. It dissolves into air in tasks and telephones and trips to the store. You need time not to write, in order to write. A whole day, for three or four hours. Time to consider. And time not to think about what you are writing. Time to walk around in a circle. You may be sweeping the floor, or doing laundry. But you need that time for your characters to develop a tone that's consistent, and a strong clear heart. I had a client once who wanted to write a book called *Finding Time,* but she never could. She would do outlines that took her months, far longer than they should have. In the end, she never found time. She was a sociologist who specialized in time and how it's used. She sent me a note one day, a note she squeezed in between grading papers and caring for her two-year-old daughter. She just couldn't find time, she painfully explained. And she knew she never would.

I know what she means. But Harbinger Singh (you Babu, you Tex) seems to have found it. Found it, and given it its rightful place: to use for his revenge (whatever that may turn out to be). Ana in Admiration

She moved toward the kitchen to drink a glass of water. She took out a bright red glass from her very small and precarious shelf, a glass she'd found years ago at a Goodwill in Delaware. Full of water, the glass looked as though it held a rich, red drink, startling and strong, with an unforgettable taste. She closed her eyes, and tried to imagine the glass contained an actual potion that could, in minutes, transform her to a chain-smoking Czechoslovakian novelist whose novels revealed a faith in love, in country, and in human kindness in the face of ever-increasing political disillusionment. Black and engaging.

Although this was not easy, she could picture the novels if she tried hard enough, their keen irony, their naive, lyrical timber, and their stories, so rich, so transforming, that no one who read them would ever be able to forget what she'd written. Never.

Dear Arlette Rosen,

I see *Auschwitz Everywhere*. (That is the title of my new work in progress.)

My family are Quakers. I am a Buddhist. That is a more unusual circumstance than you might suppose.

Auschwitz Everywhere is my own deeply probing meditation on memory, language, and epistemology. I don't know why I see Auschwitz everywhere. I just do.

Is this a book?

I understand you know such things.

Ann Wald.

17

indian boxers

Arlette kept a file called Favorite Letters. They were letters with the strongest, clearest voices, that told stories she hadn't heard before. They were often funny, full of an energy and a rawness that drew her to them. Although she didn't often work on the books they described.

They were voices always around her. The way music surrounded musicians, and colors often filled a painter's life, she saw herself in a world of words, words on paper, rather than spoken, preferably written by hand.

As a child, she began a postcard collection. She didn't collect pictures, but the handwritten messages that people wrote to one another. In the junk stores she went to very often with her mother, she would read note after note about vacations, about sickness, even death, about love and plans. They were usually written with dark black ink, an ink that stayed alive years after the writer died. She loved the sentences, and the hands that made them. She imagined people writing, in small rooms everywhere, sending friends small pieces of a story. Imagining those stories occupied much of her childhood. She kept the postcards in shoeboxes. Thousands of them still sat in her mother's attic. And she still bought them.

Dr. Thomas Do's letter went in the FL file. She reread it while she waited for Harbinger Singh. She knew he was on his way.

Dear Miss Rosen:

Scores of creatures you've never considered, some poisonous, and one that squirts blood from its eye, are becoming the focus of a new international movement, Brown Up. Intended to save creatures who are among the world's most ignored varieties, this movement was started by the undersigned (Dr. Thomas Do), after 30 years in the Mojave Desert, where I founded the International Desert Lizard Preservation Committee.

These brown animals are ignored for several reasons. 1) They don't have big, sad eyes. 2) They are not conventionally handsome. 3) They are not heroes and heroines in children's books, because of their weird looks.

Brown Up, the book and the movement, is intended to correct this long-standing prejudice by providing documentation, both historical and literary, of all these animals whose rights the movement covers, all animals in any kind of sand. Complete with relevant quotations from famous people ranging from Aristotle to Zebulon Pike, this groundbreaking collection will also have

pictures so the reader will be able to identify a
horned lizard, a desert toad, and more or less
everything else in the Brown category. People are
tired of saving whales. They're looking for
something new.

A zoologist by profession, I am not a writer, per
se. It's in that part of the process that I need
your help. I understand you work by mail. How? Can
I pay with a credit card?

Enclosed are several photographs of my two
favorite horned lizards, Cain and Abel. They are
family pets.

Yours,

Dr. Thomas Do

Harbinger too had his fantasies. Although his vacillated
wildly, he often saw himself poised on an urban mountaintop, part Gandhi, part Elvis, part mountain itself. In his
dream, he was a majestic and articulate hero, a hero of burn-
ing authority, desperate eloquence, a complex train of
thought, and a basic simplicity, a purity and honesty that
never could be questioned. He imagined he was startlingly
handsome, Omar Sharif and Billy Dee Williams. In this fantasy, he often wore a shiny black bikini, very different from
his red plaid swim shorts that Carla called Indian boxers.
And if he was being completely honest, which was not his
way, he'd admit to wanting a woman right there with him on
the ubiquitous mountaintop, a powerful woman, more or less
his equivalent, a Supreme Court judge, perhaps, or even a
high priestess and judge combined, a woman of infinite erotic
imagination, very large breasts, and a startling vocabulary,
with a face, both beautiful and kind, that evoked reverence,
devotion and respect.

Harbinger decided to invite Arlette to dinner. He chose the hour to call when an affirmative answer would be most likely, three p.m. on the dot, and then he dialed. He'd learned this technique in taxes. Mid-afternoons, most clients felt a lessening of energy and the will to resist. In the mornings, or at night, it was easier to fight.

Generally, Harbinger believed that most people answered on the second or third ring, but it took five for Arlette to pick up. Where was she, he wondered. Could she have guests? If so, why not her machine? He knew the size of her apartment, the number of steps it would take to get from corner to corner. Measuring in numbers was his life.

Her voice was small and breathy. For a minute, he imagined that he'd called Marilyn Monroe. He, Harbinger Singh, had picked up the phone and dialed his Marilyn at three p.m. one Tuesday afternoon, one two three. He deepened his voice.

"Why hello there," he said to her breathy hello, hoping those words sounded masculine and mellow.

Arlette appeared a little confused. "May I ask who this is? Do I know you?"

"Why of course," said Harbinger. His voice cracked between *of* and *course*.

"Harbinger," she said, more like herself. "I didn't know you for a minute. I wasn't expecting your call. It's not your slot. I'm sorry."

"You too,' he replied. "I imagined you were Marilyn Monroe." And then he blushed, grateful there was no way she could see him.

"That's right, Marilyn," he added, so that she wouldn't think he was just flattering her so she'd go to dinner. "I was wondering. You may think this an odd request. I suppose it is. But it's well intentioned. I have no devious and unforeseen motives. It's a completely spontaneous call. Spontaneity is not really my way. Spontaneous taxes are antithetical ideas. If I left the business of taxes for people to handle whenever they felt the urge, no one would. That might not be such a bad thing. Don't ever tell anyone I said that. I'm babbling, I know. I will stop. Right here and now. Will you go with me to dinner? You can pick the night and the food. It's your company I'd like. Just that." And then he coughed.

She wasn't sure. She wanted to go. But was it right?

"I'm not very spontaneous either," she replied. "But yes."

Dear Arlette,

Have I got an idea for you! And I mean business!

I'm talking endless possibilities! I don't just mean TV! I mean board games! Maybe even a calendar! In the right hands, this could really take off! KaBoom!

Someone with insight could see what I'm talking about! I understand that Insight could be your middle name. Don't ask who told me. He said that in the end you weren't the best of friends. These things happen. He's not such an easy guy. And maybe his idea wasn't worth all that much. After all, how big an audience is there (if we're being all that honest) for a science fiction series in Yiddish? *Oy Vey an Alien!* is some title, though. Didn't you think he had the material to work with? I'm not sure about *Outer Space Rabbis and Rebbitzens*. But maybe, if one of them committed a murder, you'd have something. The holiest rabbi. He'd see an injustice and Wham. Maybe Mel Brooks would buy it for the movies.

My idea is a little different. I hope you're sitting down. And if you're not, I invite you to take this opportunity. *Faggot Kike: A True Story*. That's right. He gave me permission. I know him well. It will be anonymous as told to (me). He's a

gay Rabbi in Nome, Alaska, and he's ready to tell
his story. For years I told him Go Ahead. But
then, he wasn't ready and now he is. We can move
Nome to Anchorage if we wanted. Or even Hawaii.
The place doesn't matter. But what a story. His
mother, his lovers, the rabbinate, the
congregants. The whole thing. Remember the big
success of that book about Lesbian Nuns fishing in
New Zealand? If that did well, just imagine!

I am a Writer-Rabbi myself, with a small
congregation in northeast Connecticut. (I am
Heterosexual.) I have written a successful series,
How To Celebrate (Rosh Hashanah, Yom Kippur,
Passover, Purim, Succoth, Simhat Torah, etc.,
published by Tel Aviv Books). But I need help with
this. We want big. Not that Tel Aviv's so small.
What do you think? I'm anxiously waiting.

Yours in Peace, Samuel Geffner, Rabbi

18

it skips a generation

Arlette's grandmother called early Sunday mornings, usually around eight. She lived in California, two doors down from Rosemary Clooney's mother. Her name was Adella. Adella woke up at five, no matter what. She liked to do her calling when she felt at her strongest. She would do her chores in the morning, clean a little, watch some TV, read Dear Abby, and prepare a very light lunch. And then she'd nap and wake up ready for the girls. The girls were all seventy-five-plus. They met every afternoon, in a hotel lobby in Beverly Hills, a stately place that served apple crumb cake, lemon in neat wedges, and seven kinds of tea. They liked the lobby not only for the tea, but mainly because there were always quartets: groups of chamber musicians playing music that was familiar, classical pieces they remembered from childhood. All of them were from the same Romanian village. Sixty years later, they lived in a four-block radius in Los Angeles.

"Arlette," Adella said in her soft and definitive voice. Her r's trilled gently. People who didn't know thought she must be a native French speaker, because her accent was almost French. "Arlette, my child. I hope I didn't wake you. But if I did, I'd rather not know. Guilt is overrated," she said. "I don't want it. I have enough. Your Uncle Manny. It's not my fault. He tells me his therapist thinks so. Did I tell him to marry Doris? And then that Michelle with her leather-thonged bikini? But what can his therapist know? Only what he tells her. Is that fair? You tell me. I don't think so. One side is all she has. One side of anything is half. Sometimes less. How are you Bubbele?" she said. "You can tell me. I know a little bit about life. And besides that, I'm your grandma. If I don't love you absolutely, you can shoot me. You know I do."

Usually Arlette answered with a kind of distant enthusiasm. She described a movie she might have seen, or told Adella about her mother, or told a story about someone she'd seen on the street. But she rarely discussed how she felt. Not because she didn't love her—Adella was Arlette's favorite relative—but because she had the feeling that once she started, she'd never be able to stop. So she just didn't begin.

"Fine, Grandma, fine," she replied.

"You sound *shlach*. Not so good. What's wrong? You can tell me. You want to get married, is that it? Marriage is no big deal. Not really. Anyone can do it, and they do. In this country, they make a big deal out of everything. Everything is a profession. If you want to get married, you go talk to someone about it. If you are fighting with your neighbor, you talk to someone. There's an expert for everything. I should have the money those people make. If you want to get married, go buy a new hat. That's what I used to tell my sisters. Rose was happy with Jack may he rest in peace. Not Bessie. Bessie married Max and we all said she was crazy. But she wouldn't listen. Even Mama. I remember she told us there wasn't a lot of knocking at Bessie's door. About Bessie, you couldn't tell her a thing. She knew. Some people are like that. I don't think she had one happy day. Still they had the children. Not that they're specimens either. But she wouldn't leave her Max. Though she had reasons. Are you busy? It's nice to be busy," she said.

"Busy enough," answered Arlette. "I have my work. I go to the movies. I have friends," she said, and thought of Jake.

"Anyone special?" Adella asked.

"Just Jake," Arlette replied.

"If there's a just, he's not. Special is no just," she said. "Special is special. Xavier Cougat. Itzhak Perlman. Eartha Kitt. Jack Benny. Golda Meir. Harry Belafonte. Marilyn Monroe. They're special. You don't have to think twice. You don't need an expert or a consultant. Imagine consulting a specialist to find out if someone is special. That would really be something," she said, and laughed.

"Grandma," said Arlette. "How are you?"

"Me?" Adella answered, with a smile in her voice. "I am fine. Just fine. I have my friends. I have my life. I live on a street with thirty-eight flavors. I saw Kim Novak in the supermarket two nights ago. Beautiful. A little overweight, but beautiful. My life is simple. I don't ask for much. I'm happy with what I have. But you," she added. "You're still young. You should ask for a lot. A lot you deserve. You're a smart girl. A nice face. A good heart. The world is your oyster, if you'll excuse the expression."

137

"I'll try," Arlette replied, reduced somehow to sounding like an eleven-year-old in just a matter of minutes. "I'll try my best."

"You're my favorite," said Adella. "Don't forget. They say it skips a generation. So there's you and there's me. Maybe you should go to graduate school. It can't hurt. Keep it in mind, Bubbele. And by the way, so goodbye."

19

harbingering

The moon was an auspicious three-quarters full on the Tuesday that Harbinger met Arlette for dinner. She'd wanted to meet him at the restaurant, but he'd insisted on calling for her at home the way he imagined it was done in some more elegant and proper time, in the melodramatic movies he preferred.

It was a sticky July evening, one of those air-shaft nights that smelled like rotting garbage and stagnant water, with a very occasional jasmine waft. The city itself was a dull, wet gray, the gray of unalterable dampness.

The streets were full. People played games on the street, cards and chess and monte and backgammon, and children played around hydrants with great abandon. Trucks festooned with pink plaster elephants, stuffed brown bears, snarling tigers and turtle-warriors went by every few minutes ringing innocent-sounding bells, bells that alluded to ice creams, large and soft, like melting hills. A smaller truck, graffitied with cheerful cones of ices colored with blue and red rainbow syrups, played a tinny and compelling circus medley. Tired parents ran into the dank, close streets, willing to pay what was necessary for a minute or two of smooth, sweet coolness, a coolness that covered the other smells with the imagined smell of childhood in summer.

Harbinger walked hopefully through these hot streets to Arlette. He thought, as he walked, of his own childhood on the noisy, rich streets of Bombay, and of the easy transition from Bombay to Queens, a transition that seemed to occur overnight. In Queens, as a young teenager, he kept to himself. Even his games were silent. He did crossword puzzles, read science fiction, and wondered, on occasion, about his fate. The radio was his constant, in Bombay and Queens both. Elvis sang through the background of his life. He had older brothers, men who formed a ragged, nearly invisible border around his life. Brothers he never saw, but who he knew existed. He had many other relatives too, and a family so big it was easy to forget them. Aunts and uncles and scores of cousins, cousins he'd sometimes pass on the street, and they would just keep going. He wondered if it was indifference, or just the vagueness he knew was characteristic of his family.

His parents were formal and a little distant. He didn't know either one of them. He'd been born late, and they were tired. Too weary for Harbinger, or very much else. He imagined them waving good-bye from the deck of a big white ship, not blowing kisses or yelling goodbye, but standing in a stately manner, discreetly flashing one white handkerchief between them, up and down some requisite number of times. His mother might have read the right number somewhere, in a magazine piece, or a book.

Sometimes it surprised him how little they had to do with his life, how rarely they appeared to him, even in his dreams. His father had been dead for eleven years now, but even alive, he had been a shadowy man, not there enough to pin down. His father had worked hard. A bookkeeper for a friend from Bombay who imported brass and beads and cheap cotton clothing, he'd worked six days a week for very little money. Sometimes he worked on Sundays too. And his mother, neat and busy, even alone was full of tasks, of baskets of laundry and clothing to sort, lentils to wash, papers to discard.

For all practical purposes Harbinger felt he had no past. At least, no past to speak of. He was Indian in a way he couldn't pinpoint. He liked some of the food, but so did the entire East Village of Manhattan. He was not religious. He did not read books with Indian heroes, with handsome men and sariied women, living exotic lives. He supposed he was American somehow, or at least as much as others he saw, the scores of people of every shape and color who came to him for their taxes.

Carla was more American, maybe. She was born in Ohio, though she rarely went back. She too had relatives, but like his, they were a distant dream. Vague stories of blacksmiths, and canning tomatoes. When Carla talked about her past, she talked about apple pies. And when anyone asked her a more direct question about what her family was actually like, she said they lived Methodist lives, as though that was explanation enough for all that came before.

Carla had brothers and a sister with families of their own. But they were all far away, in Michigan and Washington and Alaska. Names on a Christmas card. One of the things they had in common was the vagueness of their pasts, empty expanses of uncertain histories and inconsequential memories. This was how he understood most American stories, even his. No beginnings, only a long middle dangling across a century or two.

Harbinger walked toward Arlette with an expectation that something pleasant might happen. He even felt buoyant. But in her lobby, his buoyancy was tempered by a couple he heard fighting. An ageless woman, not young enough or old enough, long-haired and tired, her eyes glassy, said to a man who seemed exhausted himself, "I am sick of humoring you. Of catering to your whims. So what that you're a composer. I suggest you compose a completely new life. New melody. New score. No me." Her tone was a kind of white fury. She was so enraged she spoke a little too quietly, almost in a whisper. Harbinger could barely hear her, but the force of her words, in spite of her low voice, pushed them out his way. For one brief and painful moment, he wondered if she was addressing him. Then she left the building right out the door, not briskly, but with an apathetic gait, unsure of herself, like someone unaccustomed to getting her own way. Her composer did not follow her. Instead, he stood there looking at Harbinger for a reaction.

"Women," Harbinger said in a noncommittal voice, not knowing quite why. And then he had a sense that more was required. "You can't predict them," he added, hoping the composer would take this as comfort.

"Goddamn fucking bitch," said the man, looking right into Harbinger's eyes. "I'd like to kill her. I don't care if she lives or dies. On top of that, she's got a tin ear. We have nothing in common. Just nothing." And then he walked out the door, in a very unruffled fashion. As if he was going to a large and cheerful party.

This upset Harbinger, who felt as if the woman's venom had been directed at him. Was he a burden? Was she a psychic who could see straight into his soul? Would she be back? Did she know Carla? Or Arlette? Did she know he was secretly slovenly, and sometimes slept in his clothes?

He walked slowly up the stairs to Arlette's apartment, and to regain his good humor he hummed "Don't Say Nothin' Bad about My Baby," a song he unaccountably liked. Particularly the part that went "Uh Huh." And by the time he reached Arlette's door, his mood was restored.

He practiced hellos a few times, but decided to sing. When she opened her door, he sang the song straight through, gesturing with his hands in the broad convincing manner he remembered from a Dick Clark show years before, a show where he, a boy in Queens, watched beautiful black women with a lustfulness and envy he couldn't remember feeling since. Those women were somehow more real to him than Carla. They were so beautiful, so spangled and alive, with their big round asses and their grace. But what he really loved about them was the smoothness of their singing. Maybe he could find a woman like that. Or maybe he himself could really learn to sing. He could take lessons. Maybe he could turn himself into a rapper. He'd call himself the Tax Man. It might catch on.

He'd like to learn how to move, too. To be fluid and graceful. To flow forward instead of being all knotted up in other people's numbers, numbers even he knew didn't matter very much. Numbers that pretended to represent whole lives.

Arlette smiled while Harbinger sang. Then she stepped into the hall herself, and opened her arms wide. "He wore tan shoes and pink shoelaces," she began, pointing down at her feet. Harbinger moved back a little bit to get a better view of her rendition. He knew the song.

Arlette looked like a professional, like one of those thin gymnasts with unisex associates he'd seen on MTV. Taut and free, able to execute those fancy steps he saw them do out of the corner of his eye. Those carefully orchestrated steps to their freedom.

Arlette didn't look like Haldora or Yvette. She was suddenly Honey, or Mamie, or Beauty, or Aretha. He wondered what she'd think if he told her that, but quickly decided against it. It was probably not politically correct.

"Hello," he said. "Just for tonight," he said, "I would like to be Little Richard. Not be him exactly, but to think of myself in his shoes. As though I could belt out "Long Tall Sally." A geometric hairdo maybe, and a bright green jacket that shimmers." He was wearing a beige drip-dry summer suit, something the salesman laughingly said he could wear into the shower.

"And you?" he asked.

"It's about time I was someone else," she replied, and her voice seemed to loosen just a little. "I think I'll be," she said, and paused, uncertain. "I'm not sure which way to go."

Then adamantly he declared, "Don't chose someone I've never heard of. Some obscure intellectual who wrote an important article about God knows what. Feminism and the common cold. You have to know what I'm talking about there. Go for soul," he said, smiling in an all-knowing way. "Forget about the rest. It doesn't matter. Sophia Loren, for instance. It's just a suggestion."

"Of course you're right," she said. "I would rather be someone in a tight red dress with a closet full of feather boas. Someone with a recognizable scent." She picked up her bag to leave, and Harbinger kept talking.

"What's a scent?" he asked. They walked across town and down, to a restaurant called Jewel, one of those places that calls itself intimate yet continental. All-encompassing. "I've always wanted a long, black beard," he continued.

"Why don't you just buy one in a costume shop? They don't just have Santa beards. I'll bet a good store would have a lot of different kinds."

"But what about the string?"

"Just pretend it isn't there. And if anyone acts like you're crazy, stare them down."

They found talking very easy. It was not labored hours that each of them had feared, with difficult, halting slowness, a forced scramble for comfortable topics, arrhythmic moments of awkward attempts that often seem a little bit better than silence. They did not fall in love, or feel the charge that sometimes comes from uncertainty. But they enjoyed themselves. It was not exciting in the usual way. There were no sparks, no life-changing moments, no deep and longing looks, eye to groin, the usual whirlpool of innuendo and hope. They were not, for all practical purposes, a couple with any particular mission.

During the meal, Harbinger had moments of humming. His humming choices were broad, from *South Pacific* to Ravi Shankar. Arlette felt a kind of light energy, maybe from his songs, or her own. At her insistence, Harbinger described his favorite audits, audits he'd won, on one technicality or another. And Arlette, too, told her stories. Books she loved. They listened quietly to one another, more eager to hear than to tell their own stories. After brandy and dessert, Arlette asked Harbinger if he wanted to talk about Carla.

"Not on your life." He began to tell her how he knew that a novel that called itself *At the Bench,* or *On the Bench,* or even *Near the Bench* had the audience he wanted. He told her he wanted his own TV show, and a whole word named after him, *harbingering,* which would mean winning with a certainty that was absolute. He wanted to go on television talking about his book and then his movie, so his mother, a silent old lady living in dreams in her very small Queens apartment, would suddenly see him the way she'd always wanted him to be, an Indian Burt Reynolds, maybe, charming, successful, able to get what he wanted just by asking.

Arlette lied to Harbinger, but she did so happily. She suggested that her mother would like her to be Gertrude Stein, learned, interesting, able to make poetry from all she saw. But probably not gay.

Harbinger took Arlette home in a taxi. The space was awkward, too close to have the room they each needed without making an obvious point. The good will between them wasn't lost when Arlette suggested, a few blocks from her house, that Harbinger just keep going, that she was fine walking up by herself. She hummed a few bars of "Good Night, Irene," and he hummed "Good Night" right back.

20

submission den

From: Submission Den

To: Arlette Rosen

Some people think we have something to do with S &
M. Not at all.

We are a service for people like YOU, people who
have POEMS, ARTICLES, STORIES, PLAYS, and
SCREENPLAYS to submit and are Just Too Busy. As
well as possibly burned out, frightened,
disorganized, and unsure.

We'll submit for you. Free yourself to write. For
info. (Fees, and a brochure.)

Your Writing Aide, Yorik Blumenfeld

POB 12345, Grand Forks, North Dakota

Jake's office was painted a color he called movie-frame black. He liked to think of his space as one frame, a dense story, unseeable, except under a rare kind of lens. He saw himself as the kind of artist who could only expand in very small spaces, who needed both historical and physical constraints. Within them, he could feel his own freedom. He thought of his space not as controlled but ordered, with good reason.

He wrote with black pencils. He did not use the orangey Crayola kind, the number twos that everyone else seemed to accept. He wrote away for his, to a pencil factory in Munich. Every few years or so they would send him one hundred of the only pencils he would use. Pens too. He liked his tips micro-fine, and his ink, only black, was also precise. Night Black, they called it. That too, he ordered, but from London.

He'd insisted on blackness for years. The women around him, and there'd been a few, always protested after a while, though at first they'd been intrigued. He had changed women more easily than blackness. After a while, they all gave him colors that weren't his. They bought him navy ties with patterns, and brown-laced shoes. He disliked ties and shoelaces and zippers, all those details that seemed to get in his way. He admired what he referred to as Italian Smoothness, though even he wasn't sure whether or not this idea was real. He lived by many rules. Jake stacked his books horizontally, never vertically, on his desk. The ficus plant in his office was only watered with what he referred to as "natural water." He meant rain. Jake was always in control, more or less. Though he wasn't. His screenplay was taking forever. And even at its best, in those scenes he rewrote over and over again, when his hero/antihero Joe LaMothe arrived in town, for instance, LaMothe couldn't seem to enter the bar with the ominous forcefulness that Jake intended. He just walked in, no matter how hard Jake tried. He knew, in a way, that the screenplay had a kind of flatness to it, like the flatness of any bad movie. Even so, he couldn't leave it. Not until it was done.

This screenplay, so much a part of who he was, was still very far from Jake's idea of what a movie might be, a luminescent ninety minutes made memorable for the way dreamlike images floated sometimes to a true and eerie music. A way that seemed more magical than anything. Kurosawa was his god.

Jake didn't float. He didn't know how. He was tethered not only to earth, but to his own endless rules. He wished he dreamt about talking chickens. He wished he could throw away what he believed and start over. He wanted another chance, but he didn't know how to go about getting one. Once he'd lived with a woman who spent all her time laughing or crying. He'd wanted to kill her. He couldn't believe he'd been foolish enough to be with her in the first place, they were so ill-suited. And yet, he somehow felt that she cried and laughed for him too. It took a long time for them to fall apart, but it hadn't been the usual floating away that he knew well. Instead, she shrieked, she broke things, she took his good black Italian suit and cut it into small pieces.

He wished there were a book he could read, a film he could see, something he could do that would change him, unlock what he knew must be there. He hated self-help, hated people who sat in circles confessing. He felt he had nothing to confess, and still he wanted to be able to feel something he didn't first have to consider. He knew he was always looking for a point of certainty, a place he could use to start his own world. But that point eluded him, and he didn't know quite how to get there. Sometimes he believed this point didn't matter, that films, with their magic, were a good enough center. But was it enough just to see them? He read a quote somewhere from Henry Moore, which said that life's trick was to find work that was your passion, work you related to completely, and could never finish.

He did not believe in himself entirely. He knew there was not enough magic in him to do, in the end, what it was he wanted, to make a film from the center of his soul. The kind of film he admired. He hoped one day to write at least one scene—maybe that would be enough—so full of the magic he saw when Marcello Mastroianni danced with Anita Ekberg around the Piazza Navona in *Eight and a Half*. He needed years of drugs to set him free, of liquor end to end, or maybe a guided mediation. He saw the world, but in a way which he found hard to translate into the kind of storytelling he admired, scenes which had their own life, which had breadth and resonance and a melody. Scenes which felt like an eastern European novel, all angst and charm, visionary and powerful, with a subtle and underlying wit. And with the knowledge, somehow, of holocausts and wars, of Tolstoy and Gertrude Stein, and of images that move forward on their own.

Jake thought he wanted Arlette. He knew she could love him. And he could love her, too. But they formed a kind of quiet harmony when they were able to give up their fighting. Suddenly, he just wanted to hear her voice. "Hello," he said. Just hello.

"Jake?" she seemed to doubt even his voice. He could have been a stranger, someone who wanted, more than anything in the world, to write a book about anything. Pick a book. Any book. *Anarchy Explored*. *The Real Truth about Sigmund Freud*. *Antoine the Unholy*. A radish cookbook. A novel about a woman who fell in love with an owl.

"I don't know what love really means," he said, and then she knew.

"Maybe there are no words for what you want. It could be that this conversation you imagine can never take place. And never has. Not only with us. But with anyone else. Maybe the intimacy you imagine is just a myth. The material for art. Not life."

"Do you believe that?" he asked her. "That art is only artifice?"

"I think art is Harbinger Singh," she said.

"You're probably right." His voice remained low. He did not continue his tasks while he talked to her. He did not put all his pennies face side up, and slide them into rolls, or Windex the pens on his desk. He did not draw pictures of submarines, over and over, or write notes to himself about what he must do later. He did not pretend he was listening while accomplishing something else.

"But the last time we went through this, you accused me of sounding like *Fiddler on the Roof*."

"I didn't ask you if you loved me, did I?"

"Love," she said. "Do you want to know what Simone de Beauvoir said about love?"

"No," he replied. "Just no. No, I don't. I don't want to know what anyone said about it. Not Rilke. Not Roethke. Not Germaine Greer. Not Catherine MacKinnon. Not Mick Jagger. Not I. F. Stone. Not Allan Ginsberg or LeRoi Jones. Not Fellini. Not Milosz. Not Confucius or Allah or the Talmud. Not Lao Tzu or Milan Kundera or Susan Sontag or Emily Dickinson or Max Frisch or your mother!" he said, and by then he was shouting so loudly that his voice sounded like the voice of a stranger. He rested the phone handle down on the table for a minute. He could hear his own heart pounding. Something had happened, but he didn't know what.

He looked down at his hands, very pale and thin. He picked the phone back up. She was still on the line.

"I may be moving," he said, his voice back to its usual flatness. "I'm not sure where. But it's a thought I've had more than once. I could probably get a film festival job. Film festivals are a dime a dozen now. The hot dog guy on my corner was talking to me yesterday about running a hot dog festival—showing movies with hot dogs in them."

"Oh." She didn't know what else to say.

"My life here is movies and plans for dinner. I'm tired of that," he replied.

"What should it be?" she asked.

"Work that is unending," he said. "That tells the truth. That brings me a little bit closer."

"Closer to what?" she asked.

"Maybe to you," he replied. And then they both were silent for a minute.

"I'm sorry, Jake. Sorry for my distance. It's not what I want. I would like to be able to love you. In a more open way. It would be awful if you left. I want to try. I just don't know how."

"Why don't you?"

"Do you? Does anyone? I suppose some people do a better job. We try, all of us. We are trying. What I know how to do is read you the letter I got today. I'm not changing the subject. I think we should continue this conversation in an open-ended way. When we're together."

"Me too," he said. "I'd like to hear one of your letters. I'm sure you have one or two or three. Let me guess, first. A book about contradictions of family life. Or psychological intimacy. Or an interconnected cycle of stories exploring the lives of young suburban girls. Those are my three best guesses. We can talk about us later."

"Not bad guesses," she said. "They could be books. But they're not this one. I'll give you a clue. The writer calls me Sister."

"You'd better just read it."

"OK."

She often tried to read in a voice that sounded like the author's might. She often tried to picture the author: age, height, tone of voice, an odd detail here or there.

My Sister;

Broken Vessels: Women and Virginity is an argument for celibacy, from the point of view of keeping selfhood intact. As you may know, I have long argued that men should not have erections, if they want to be our equal. After all, an erection creates the problem of the penetrator and the penetratee (the doer and the doee, if you prefer). My thesis has received wide recognition, and has been debated around the world, particularly in Finland and a few of the more progressive Scandinavian countries, such as Denmark.

Broken Vessels promises to be just as controversial. Most women don't like to think of themselves as broken, after all. And we aren't really. That is, we don't have to be.

I need a certain amount of editing, and your name was on a list of Feminist Book Doctors. (This has certainly become an active profession. I was glad to see that many women appear to be accredited.)

I am writing to all of you, to ask these two questions:

1)How quick are you?

2)What is your current availability?

3)What is your philosophical relationship to text?

That is, how do you see your role?

4)How interested are you in this particular discourse?

I would appreciate your quick reply.

Sincerely,

SUSUN WOMYN

Jake spoke first. "It's probably a good idea. Who knows?" "Who does know?" she replied. "Not me."

21

dreamspert

Dear Aretha/Ivonne/Yvette/Arlette,

How about all four? Like those Southern Belles on TV. I saw one once whose name seemed to be Sue Sue Sue. Sometimes, although I have been in this country most of my life, I feel I don't hear as well as I might, and her name might not have been that at all. It could have been something like Honey Bee Sue. Though it just as well might have, too. How much TV do you watch, by the way? My guess is not enough. You look like a "*Simpsons* on occasion" type. TV could be just what you need. A little loosening.

Our dinner was worthy, I do believe, of a writing exercise. So I thought I'd try. All this exercising is giving me the feeling that I am actually writing. Am I? You let me know. You are the expert. I was a little nervous when I picked you up. And hot. These things can go either way. I've spent many a dull dinner. I know you don't think I am capable of that kind of observation. But I know dull from not. The dullest dinner I ever spent. Do you think that could be interesting? Or not? That's an example of something I just don't know. I suppose in the right hands, anything is passable. And mine aren't those hands yet.

So we went to dinner. I felt a little like a pupil with his teacher out of school. Have you ever been in that position before? I have not. I'm accustomed to keeping my relationships in their proper places. Teacher here, pupil there. That kind of thing. Tax clients, for example, are certainly not friends. Although I try to be friendly enough. I always ask how they are. But I have no thought that they're actually going to tell me. What about you? I guess that's the kind of question I should have asked at dinner.

Should I mention what we ordered? Would that be of any interest? Or not? A martini with a twist (me) a Bloody Mary with a substantial wedge of lemon (you). We each had several. And a bottle of medium-priced red wine. I like white but you seemed to want red. Did I imagine that? Salmon and steak. You and me. Should I stop with the main course, or continue with dessert? I'm going to have to decide that on my own. I'll stop. (Maybe there can be a footnote here: creme caramel, and chocolate cake.) I can hear you saying in that authoritative way of yours, a way I wouldn't question, not yet at least. But What Happened? What was the dinner about? Well this is where I am stumped. I'd have an easier time telling you if it was on TV. Not that I know all that much about TV. But somehow, the real life aspect of this is too confusing. It makes me nervous.

A Little Later (The Same Day)

Arlette,

I didn't like my first letter. But you suggested that I hold on to all my attempts, that I try to give you everything I've written. Remember my imaginary dialogue, client and tax man, where the client suddenly says, "I hate you and your stupid taxes. I hate the idea that we have to spend two hours together, two hours I pay for, where you divide my life into the most arbitrary parts, into travel expenses and home entertainment, newspaper subscriptions and charities. I hate you for that, Mr. Harbinger Singh." Well, that was one exercise I certainly wasn't planning to show you (though I did). For one thing, you have a very low picture of people who do taxes. And the matter of taxes in general. (That client could have been you.) And for another, I didn't like the idea that the client (I called her Norma Irma Birnbaum, if you remember, of NIB, for Her Nibs) was so out of control, even though you said that out of control can be interesting. (I'm not writing about serial murders, as you know. Only taxes.) I felt that the character was yelling at me, and I didn't want that. Even though I created her completely, as you know. I made her frowzy, and a little too thin. My Marla, on the other hand, is a voluptuous idea. She wears high thin heels with a come-hither sound. Her hair is abundant, too voluminous to be successfully reigned in, and she constantly smiles in an intelligent way. She's neither judging or distant. She's more or less the antithesis of Ms. Norma Birnbaum.

So what does all of this have to do with our dinner? You are probably wondering that. Well, our dinner was one of those nights that just fly by. Sometimes I feel that our writing hours do that too. What do you think causes some things to float, while others just plod along? Our dinner together was a pleasant mood, a whistled song. The details don't matter very much: my steak, your salmon. A small dark room. In fact the details might get in the way. Am I wrong? Is the song in those details? Should they be part of what I write? How important would you say they are? I would guess that my suit, for instance, could be any color and so could your dress. Unless it were orange, for instance. Which it wasn't. In *The Bench,* if I write it, the details might matter. Particularly if it's about a trial. Or would they? As always, I look to you for an answer or two. Your devoted pupil and tax consultant, HS

Dear HS,

I'm sorry to say I have no answers. I wish I did. *On the Bench, Hot and Dusty, Arguendo.* It can all be good or not, depending. But it's hard to say I liked the pieces together, and would probably suggest combining them, and using parts from each. As an exercise, perhaps. This seems like an odd thing for me to tell you, given the fact that it's the way I earn my living, but I'm just not sure. You have to trust yourself somehow, to try everything. To use your instincts, and just write as much and as often as you can. There are rules, but they don't matter. You know that anyone good enough, or charming enough, or convincing, can break what rules there are. First person novels are supposed to be taboo. But look at *Moby Dick*.

The story doesn't matter. I know you think your story is the reason you're writing. But the truth is, you're writing for revenge, which is as good a reason as any. But your revenge doesn't have to be so literal. Maybe it would be revenge enough for Carla to see you happy. Maybe she understands you as a person who is limited by something or other. But in your book, you can just prove her wrong. You can paint yourself as suave and all-knowing, a James Mason type (I'm sure there is an Indian equivalent), with a resonating baritone full of certainty and innuendo. How about that for your Harbinger character? Wouldn't a devastatingly irresistible hero be enough revenge? Of course, you can do what you want with Carla/Marla. It's your book, as we both know. But if your *Bench/Dusty* hero is good enough, if he wins the battle, uncovers the murder, or does what he's supposed to altogether, he can be a hero once again. In another book. And there, he can make passionate love for ninety-six hours with a woman who has enormous breasts, recite Plato in ancient Greek, or fall in love with a woman who has received a lifetime MacArthur for painting. Or, if you prefer, who looks like Vanna White.

It's all up to you, which is, as you know, the miracle of writing.

I must say though that I've been impressed by your imagination, and your skill. And the idea of a bright green suit. You are a wonderful Little Richard, Harbinger. Your "Long Tall Sally" was by far the best I've ever heard. I don't remember liking his version as much as I liked yours. Your singing made our meal. (And it was missing from your version of what happened. Why?) No one ever sang for me, except for my mother's "Rockabye Baby," and you might say that was predictable (though I didn't know that then). Maybe *The Bench* can have singing in it. A CD to accompany the novel. I wonder if anyone's ever done a serious trial with songs. You can have an index of the songs used, if you like. Imagine the main character singing "Long Tall Sally." I think that would endear him to the jury.

You know, Babu, your writing has affected mine. Maybe I shouldn't charge you. Though I really do think that your approach is the first original notion (but not nauseatingly so:

women falling in love with dolphins is original enough. But somehow, I hate it) that I've come across in years. Not lawyers and the bench, or even revenge, but the whole package strikes me as so un–Philip Roth. And I love Philip Roth. That's not the problem. Maybe I am mistaking your desire for revenge for art. But I don't think so. (Maybe I am mistaking you for art. Could that be?)

I am becoming Haldora-Yvette, and you have become Babu. What does that mean? I think it means that we should form a singing group, and write rap songs about our favorite books. I can begin with *Stuart Little*. Have you read it? Probably not. It's sort of a mouse liberation story. It lends itself to song. Maybe everything does.

Yours, H-Y-A

Dear H-Y-A,

I'm saving your notes (and copies of mine). I hope you don't mind that. The tax business has taught me to Xerox everything, usually twice. It may be relevant later. It's all in a file marked "Possible Revenge." I'm telling you because I think you should be aware of that when you write to me. I don't believe in surreptitiousness. It borders on espionage, which seems immoral. I'm sure you're thinking to yourself: that's an idea that's not very Singh-like. I guess in the end we are all predictable, but there's not much you and I can do about that. Or is there? I've often thought there's money to be made in altering people's dreams. Though I'm not the man for the job. Even so, I know just how the whole thing could work. Someone would come into the office (I think, somehow, it should be blue) and express their problems in the language of their choice, but the essence of the problem would always be the same: They don't like their dreams. The Dreamspert could change all that. For example, let's say I had the most ordinary of dreams: an elephant chasing me, for instance. Or falling. Say I'd had those dreams all my life. Say I was simply tired of being so locked in. The Dreamspert would listen to me for a while, and then make a suggestion. A big problem is that most people feel trapped. They can't imagine another way to go. So she might say, "Tonight you'll dream about a monkey in the Balinese monkey forest." And that suggestion is really all some people need to begin to dream about monkeys. That monkey's enough to change things around. Dreams are just suggestions. Wouldn't that be a nice job? Suggesting dreams?

By the way, if you have a problem with my Xeroxing your letters, or even with filing them, just let me know. I am not as set in my ways as I might seem. B.

Dear B.,

You don't seem as closed as all that. In fact, you seem very open. I wish I were too.

I like Xeroxing. Don't ask me why. I hate spies too. Yes, a Dreamspert would be a wonderful job. I would suggest that people dream of ringing bells. And incredible sounds, trills and bellows and Bach.

Yours, A.

Dear Arlette,

Last night I dreamt about a man named Toe who was married to a woman named Foot. It made me think that the names I've chosen for my characters are far too uninspired. Even Marla, though I've grown to like it. I'm even a little in love with it, if I were to tell you the truth.

Marla's *Hot and Dusty* sounds a little like a restaurant, maybe Mexican. More that than a novel of passion, lust, and the law. I realize now that revenge has been done. And courtrooms too, over and over. But not, dare I suggest it, toes and feet, as one small example of what could be possible. (Toe and Foot were happy, by the way. They lived in one of those beautiful houses you sometimes see in a magazine. Big windows and glasses of wine. Dramatically off center, in the woods. Their dreams were always unexpected.)

I don't want this to seem like science fiction. That may limit my audience, heaven forbid. As you know, I want to move from a book to TV. Imagine a TV series: Toe and Foot. Now that's a concept. They can be a family, with children who are all body parts (of course, some might be Verboten. But we can take that into consideration when we're writing the pilot. I think it would be perfect for FOX, don't you? A post-*Simpsons* show. You see I am changing my way of thinking. Joining the mainstream. It may be hard, I know you're thinking, to be a Bombay/Queens Indian tax specialist named Harbinger Singh and still expect to join the mainstream. Not at all, I say you. Not at all. I'll tell you the reason why. The mainstream is changing. Toe and Foot can become as commonplace as Homer and Bart. And when they do, we'll come up with something else.

In my dream, Toe and Foot were having problems. Toe was voluptuous, I must admit. (Not all ideas can change that easily.) And Foot was a handsome man, dark and sensitive, with a strong chin, and penetrating eyes. Yes I know you've heard that before too. But if I give him three beady eyes for instance, and one pointed yellow tooth extending straight out from his nostrils, no one will want to look at him, much less find him a suitable love interest. And the reader must identify. That we know.

So Toe is handsome, and Foot is beautiful. Or vice versa. In that way, they will be conventional characters. But their names will allude to something else. I can see it now: a whole big family of Arm and Leg, Tooth and Lip, Ear and Brow and Limb. They will be multicultural by definition, unisex, perfect nineties characters. They will not be gender-specific, or linked to one small tribe.

So you see, I am learning. And you thought (I could tell this from your occasionally patronizing attitude) that I was entirely fixed in my ways, confined for life, to the unimaginative dullness that you seem to believe comes from looking at numbers. And not, instead, at Great Works of Art. Is that what you do, by the way? You seem so mysterious and guarded. Is it just from me? Is it, do you think, a stance of Professional Attitude? Is that always wise?

This morning I had a client who was, if I may say so without betraying confidence, enormously straight-laced. He probably kept records of his records: of the number of times he had sex, with annotations for time, date, and place. Not to mention each phone call, each meal.

I invited him to leave the office with me, to experience a bagel and cream cheese in its natural environment. There's a place near my office, called Bagels 'n' Things. For years, I pictured myself and a client, happily smearing our cinnamon-raisin bagels with cream cheese. He ordered sesame, by the way. He was a new man in there. Much happier, let me tell you. We didn't talk about taxes at all. He was doing something new. That's the key, isn't it?

Do you like the direction I'm moving in, namewise? And in other respects? Or to you, am I just another author and book? I don't know that you'll ever tell me the truth about this. You don't seem the type. Though I live in Hope. Your Harbinger.

22

elyse

Elyse was Arlette's most graceful friend, a patient listener whose advice was always worth hearing. They'd met in college years before. Elyse often had visitors, who wanted her opinion. She became a therapist, married a psychiatrist, and moved to Montclair, right outside New York.

They did not see one another often. Elyse's life was full of a kind of busy detail that eluded Arlette: She went to meetings and conferences, saw innumerable patients, read long serious books, and only had time to schedule Arlette in very briefly. She listened more carefully than most other people, and her manner, intelligent, warm, accepting, made her the perfect audience for any sort of story.

They met in Elyse's office, a few blocks from the train. Montclair was one of those places that everybody always said was just like New York City, but it wasn't. Not at all. It was pleasant, but it didn't have any of the unpredictable chaos of a real city block. Everything about Montclair seemed even tempered. Elyse's office was a few blocks from the train station. It was neat, careful, entirely nondescript, a page from a Pottery Barn catalogue. Nothing in her office got in the way of the teller's story. There were no distractions.

A tall, very thin woman, Elyse wore clothes the color of berries. She looked loose and familiar. The women embraced and Arlette sat down in a soft, light gray couch, facing Elyse. She could feel her eyes fill up with tears. On a small glass table right next to her, there was a box of Kleenex. She grabbed one, and held it tightly.

"What is it?" asked Elyse. "Did something happen?"

Arlette couldn't talk at first. She thought she'd start to cry and never stop. She just nodded No.

"Is it Jake?" Elyse guessed. "Or something else."

"It's sort of Jake." Arlette felt her voice emerge from the back of her throat, the voice of a stranger.

"Do you want me to guess?" Elyse was always patient. "Did he do something? Did he say he wanted to leave?"

"Not at all," replied Arlette. "He would stay forever. He likes predictability more than anything. Black and white movies and the same magazines. He likes me well enough not to upset our arrangement."

"Have you met someone else?"

"Not really. I have a book client I think about a lot, more than I expected to. His name is Harbinger. He's in love with his wife and that's fine with me. I'm not even sure he knows that. But he will. She left him, and he is plotting to win her back. He loves her, and I would guess that she loves him too. They're taking a break for a while."

"I still don't see the problem here. Do you love this client?"

"I sort of do, but not in a way that makes me want to leave Jake. I love Harbinger's imagination and his energy, and the way he lives in the world. How he sees things, and what he says. Whenever he leaves, I feel that I should live a different life. That I should take risks, and be more spontaneous. That I should stop overthinking every single thing. You know, many years ago, I went to a museum with my father. I was looking at a painting for a long time—it was by Paul Klee—and my father said, "Do you know what most people are thinking when they're looking? They're thinking, 'That's nice. What time is lunch?' But that's how I am. I overthink everything. Jake has always been appropriate. Harbinger isn't. And yet, I no longer want appropriate. I want someone who can sing in my ear. And here's something else. I want to do some singing myself. Though God knows what I'd sing."

Elyse nodded, and then she stood up and walked to Arlette, and sat next to her on the couch. "This is wonderful," she said. "You are allowing yourself to struggle. Of course you should sing. How can I help you do that?"

Arlette grabbed the Kleenex. She wiped her eyes.

"You've helped me already," said Arlette. "I will sing my first song for you. But it will be 'I'm a Little Teapot,' because that's all I really know."

She started softly at first, "I'm a little teapot," barely audible the first time but, by "Tip me over and pour me out," she was nearly yelling.

23

god delivers

Arlette and Jake met on the stairs of the public library, in front of the lions. They were waiting for Harbinger Singh, but had about half an hour to wait. Jake had not been as curious as Arlette wanted him to be about the meeting, but he'd come. She wasn't even sure why she'd wanted the three of them together. Harbinger agreed without even asking who Jake was. Maybe he assumed that Jake was a potential tax client. He told her once, just in passing, that everyone was or could be. And although Arlette found this idea offensive, she hadn't minded because of the way he'd said it. Jake and Arlette were awkward together. It was the middle of an August Tuesday. Another slow, dense day, where morning and afternoon are seamlessly connected by whiteness, and time takes on another dimension, moving even more slowly, with less of the brisk efficiency of coolness. They tried to talk, but the effort was too great.

"Are you interested in the new Scorsese?" said Jake. "I've heard it's a departure."

"Not really," she said. "Though I'll go. But I find his movies too macho."

"How can a movie be macho?" he sounded a little disdainful.

"*Raging Bull* bothered me," she said. "It was so evil in a way which seems very male.

"Is male bad? Besides, it was brilliant," he said. "His best movie ever. And what editing," he added.

"Is that what matters?" she replied, but he'd already looked away.

She tried too. "Last night I had a dream about my mother. I can't remember ever dreaming about her before. Is that surprising? I don't know how often people dream about their mothers.

"She looked so young, and innocent. She told me that she'd never wanted children. I was upset, but not as upset as I would have predicted." "Hmm," he replied, so she just continued, "Do you think we should volunteer somewhere? Work one night a week in a literacy center, or a homeless shelter, or with immigrants or AIDS patients or something?"

"You sound like those white liberals and their take-a-brother-to-lunch programs," he said. "All those people who want to help. I myself suffer from compassion fatigue. The self-righteousness of it. The whole thing."

"Is there something wrong with helping?" she said.

When Harbinger appeared, they were still fumbling around, flitting over topics that might have been all right under other circumstances, that were OK enough. He brought a bag of four jelly donuts. White powder covered his fingertips. He was humming "Back in the Saddle Again," half to himself and half to them. He stopped suddenly.

"Have a donut," he said. "I am a major contributor to the Dunkin' corporation. They know what they're doing. Not many people do. With Dunkin' you get your money's worth. There aren't many other instances of customer satisfaction that I can comfortably cite. How about you? You two look as though you might prefer Krispy Kremes. Inferior, in my opinion, but passable," he said, and pointed his finger at Jake like Uncle Sam.

"Harbinger Singh, Jake Mandel," said Arlette, ignoring the question because she knew Jake had an issue with donuts. Jake himself extended his right hand in a clear straight line, out from his body the way a modern dancer might bisect his space. Neatly, poetically, with no apparent thought. Only the graceful instinct of people who move well.

"What passes for hello in your parts?" Harbinger smiled at Jake, the open smile of a self-assured cowboy in a cigarette ad. "I know *ciao* is PC goodbye, but what about hello? What is it in Swahili? Do you have any idea? I had a client who wrote an article on what to say and how to say it, taking other cultures into consideration. She sent me a Xerox. Deadly," he said, "though she makes a very nice living. That I can tell you, without betraying any particular details."

Jake smiled back at Harbinger, and moved a little closer. Arlette stood alongside them both, just watching. Saying nothing. Wondering what it was she was really watching.

"I suppose Shalom-Salaam might be OK though," he said. "Inclusive and third-world based, although these days it might be too pointed."

"What is your line?" asked Harbinger Singh. "I'm not asking for tax implications. Only curiosity." The three of them moved to sit down in the outside park behind the library, a kind of European park, open and bordered by buildings. They sat on elegant folding chairs, a table in the middle.

"Films," said Jake, continuing to smile. "It's a passion more than a field, I suppose. I love movies. Sitting in the dark with a room full of people, watching the screen. It really seems like magic, even after all these years of learning the parts. For me, in a way, it's enough that I see movies. Although, of course, I would like to believe that I will make one. In mine," he said, "the magic will be set to a music you've never heard before. It will be memorable, and moving. You'll want to see it twice. It will have no special effects. Absolutely none. It will all be a kind of raw honesty. Post-Cassavetes, post-Dogma," he said.

"Hmm," said Harbinger. And then, "I will get us all a drink. Lemonades," he explained, without asking if that would be what they wanted. He left for the kiosk, and Jake gave Arlette his who-in-the-world-is-he look. But he didn't say much. Neither did she.

I MET JAKE
AND VICE VERSA

My Arlette My Haldora Perhaps Babu should evolve into Babaloo. Or Babalooloo. That's better, isn't it. And another thing. I want a song with this. You can sing it. But I'd like my words accompanied, at all times.

And now for the body of the material. What I have taken to calling to myself, and now to you, *The Stream*. Bodies age. Streams move on.

Wouldn't you agree? (My writing is getting freer, don't you think? Pretty soon I'll be able to kill off M/Carla and move along. On the Road to Tipperary or Katmandu or Sumatra. Ha Ha Ha. I think that *Hot and Dusty* might have been a phase. Something I had to do. Like writing a first novel about my unhappy but nonetheless Indian childhood in sunny Bombay. I'm sure you are very familiar with that syndrome. It's inevitable, isn't it? All those childhood novels. No apple orchards in Flushing, Queens.

So now Jake. The music here is "Born Free." Perhaps the more vernacular way of describing the moment might be sizing each other up. Ethnic equivalents of Robert Redford and Paul Newman. More different, perhaps. Taxes and film are both fields of logic. You might disagree. Film is an art, and taxes might be a craft.

And yet there we were, easily discussing a series of subjects we had in common. Such as summer, the season we now are experiencing. He likes it, and so do I. And then, of course, donuts.

I liked Jake, not that it matters. But for the sake of this exercise, I would like to plainly state that this Jake, who seems appropriately named (part Jackal, part Rake, might be why), appears to be amiable, and personable. In my own vernacular, I might call him A Good Return. How's that for a title, by the way? It could be my version of *The Long Goodbye*. Or, I could write about M/Carla coming back (to do her taxes, and then . . . those passionate moments, hot and dusty).

I fear I have rambled. I am interested in using that extra part of my mind that deals with something other than information. I want to start the wheels turning (if I may). Yours, mine, those wheels of others. My clients, for example, are largely in need of a spin.

I think I will sign this with an all-encompassing B. (which could even be, heaven forbid, Bob).

Dear B. (unBob)

I don't know that you captured you and Jake, but you did capture something. You seem at last to be writing. Really writing. What is that, I wonder? To me, writing is learning how not to be afraid, how to be open, how to see and feel and hear. How to reveal secrets. Anaïs Nin (do you know who she is? She is controversial now, but she wasn't when I was reading with an avidity I've lost a little). Anaïs Nin said that writing is a generosity of the spirit, a jousting with energy, loving others, and giving away all of oneself to others, to celebrate life.

That seems like a lot, doesn't it? More than enough, anyway. For today. I'm glad you liked Jake. He liked you too. I have mixed feelings about Male Bonding, but I guess it's better to bond than not to.

H.

Singing "Whistle a Happy Tune," Harbinger began the walk from his office in the East 50s through the park, on his way to Arlette. He carried a Samsonite briefcase, steely gray and middle-priced, the kind he'd come to associate with taxes. On occasion he called it the anti–Steve McQueen. McQueen, he knew, if he carried a briefcase, would carry a slick black leather. Not Harbinger, who wanted to convey anything but speed, and chases. Anything but danger. HGS, in press on block letters, was centered near the top. Harbinger's middle name was actually Tagore, but he'd never liked it. In law school, he began to use G as a middle initial. Just G. When anyone asked, he said it was for George. And if that answer was still not quite enough, he'd say, as though he were able to tell a long story through one perfect word: British. This "British" was intended as an adequate George explanation. He wanted the G, not to belong exactly—for this he never truly considered—but to be acceptable in some way. To make his life as easy as he could.

He had a vague idea of smoothness, of things going well, of a kind of order and logic that led naturally to elevation. Like Bach and music. If the right numbers were found for his columns, he could make them add up to more. He often imagined a life of simple ease. He could even imagine playing golf. He would, in this perfect imagined life, sit at his desk for five hours a day, exactly. Eight to one. Harbinger was an early riser, even on weekends when he'd been married. He always had a plan: a list. He did not think of his lists as anticreative. *Au contraire*. He knew that they were riddles, puns, masterpieces made from hidden confessions masked as logic. July 11: post office, Xerox, lemons, book. This last, this book of his, was what he wanted most. *Why* was another question. And one he couldn't honestly answer. As a child of seven or eight, he wrote a poem. He remembered only his very first line: His lips were upside down. His mother listened to his poem, though she didn't seem to care much why his hero's lips were distorted. His mother was always busy. He never knew what she was doing.

After all these years, that's all he remembered: those upside-down lips, her lukewarm response. He walked quickly through the park, thinking in a way that struck him as dense. "I should keep a notebook of words," he said to himself. Words like *agog,* which have the power to evoke. Tax professionals are rarely agog. That is, they don't allow themselves to be. "Oh my God. You owe a fortune. How in the world did that happen?" He imagined himself crossing in front of his neat and careful desk, standing too close to a very nervous couple. They'd forgotten. They'd overlooked. One, he imagined, sold expensive lofts in Soho. Wealthy artists were her clientele. And her husband, a careful designer of calendars and yogurt containers, well groomed with neat white nails, owed eighteen thousand dollars in back taxes. He let himself laugh. He howled until the tears came into his eyes. And they left his office shaken.

Of course that was a fantasy, a kind of tax pornography. He never moved from behind his gray desk, no matter what. Even the day that Carla had come and asked for another chance. She hadn't asked in just that way. She hadn't even said she missed him. Just that she wanted his advice. But he'd hardly looked up. "Maybe you should make an appointment," was what he said. "I've got an audit in the morning. It's in Brooklyn. I'm not ready."

"I see," she'd said. But he noticed that she was wearing a new pale blue suit, and her hair looked purposefully ordered. She had a secret beauty, pressed down, but there in front of you if you looked hard enough.

Still, he dismissed her, as though she were anyone else. For instance, Thomas Peters, a man with a plant store on 75th and Third. Harbinger was Thomas Peters's lawyer, although they did very little for each other.

Carla looked surprised. He supposed she was accustomed to his deference, his constant acquiescence. Subservience in the face of desire. Long evenings of his nodding, half-listening to her theses about the Democratic Party and where it could possibly be going. Still he wanted Carla, for all of her speeches, for all her endless discussions of reform. He wanted Carla not because she was the most interesting person he'd ever met or even because she was particularly beautiful. Or witty or clever. Or even very firm. Carla was not firm. He knew women, and men too perhaps, were these days expected to be firm. Carla had her soft spots of flesh, her hidden pink excesses. Harbinger liked them, and liked the way they were relatively secret. Carla's clothing was often official.

It looked as though it had been drawn onto her with an engineer's ruler, and a blue Bic pen. All at right angles, all very neat. Not so.

Harbinger walked quickly. He looked around the crowded summer fields, and imagined, for once, he was on the way to a concert. Nina Simone or Emmy Lou Harris. Maybe he should take Arlette to hear music, or to see a soccer game.

By the time he'd arrived on the west side of the park, an area he thought of as the Left Bank somehow, not far from Arlette's apartment, Harbinger was nearly skipping. He hummed the *Addams Family* theme song to himself. For a minute or two, he pictured Uncle Fester as an IRS auditor. But he quickly abandoned that idea. It was a little too predictable.

"Arlette," he said, by way of hello. "Maybe if they changed the soccer rules, more people would go. Are you interested in soccer? I've wondered about that. If they eliminate the goalie, there'd be more points. So instead of two to one, the game could be eighty-nine to ninety. People like points. I'm sure of that. It's part of the general trend toward big numbers. I've watched this happen for years. Big is always good, except for poundage."

She looked as though she didn't understand him, really didn't know what he was saying, or why. But she looked a little friendlier than usual, too. Maybe a hair. "The idea itself isn't bad, I don't think, but I've never seen a real soccer match so I wouldn't actually know," was her noncommittal reply. "Maybe you'd like to come in."

"Why yes," he said, swinging down her hall with vast gashes into the air with his arms. He could have been swimming. "And now," he said, breathing deeply, "The Tao of taxes. I am ready. You see that I have been giving our work a considerable amount of thought. I am evolving. I can feel it. I am moving off the small prosaic dime that once framed the bulk of my thoughts."

"To what?" she asked, in a tone of voice implying that she already knew his answer.

"To a quarter, perhaps," he responded, then laughed. "A soccer quarter. It's all of a piece. The next thing you know, I'll be writing about the Catholic Church. Even God."

"God?"

"You know I've noticed many delivery trucks lately with 'Guaranteed Overnight Delivery' painted on the sides. It seems to be a trend. God Delivers. I wonder if that's the implicit message there. That God, in his or her way—don't think I don't know about the her—can come through. Although I must say that's not a point of view I share.

"What's happened to you today?"

"I feel unauthorized, in a way, as though I am, for this hour and forty-five minutes, finally free. When I sit within that cubicle—not that this isn't a cubicle too," he said, looking around him sweepingly, "I feel a kind of inhibition I've only recently come to know. I'm trapped in there," he said. "It could very well be that *Marla's Bench* or whatever it turns out to be could break me out of there. At least, for the duration of its pages. Do you think that borrowed lives is too much of a formula, by the way? I'm not afraid of formulas. If they can work. I haven't thought of a plot exactly, but the idea would be that someone, a Nick Nolte type I guess, would live someone else's life. He looks like he'd be good at that." Here he took a deep breath, and leaned back into a blue navy Morris chair, the chair he always sat in. He turned his whole body around to Arlette.

"You are quiet today. What's going on with you? I heard someone say that on TV. It sounded so unbelievably American that I wrote it down in my notebook. To use it later.

And here I am. Here it is." Then he laughed. "That's a reason for notebooks. I noticed recently that I've written 'Have a Good One' many times."

"I can't keep up with you today," she said, and stood up from her own predictable faded brown leather desk chair she'd dragged up from the street, years ago. "But I do have something to give to you. First I'd like to read you a paragraph. You asked me a while ago, maybe the first time we met, what made me a writer. And I felt I didn't answer you properly. So I've written you an answer. I'd like to read it out loud. I don't entirely like reading out loud because the words can sound wrong. They can seem hollow. Reading is very different from writing. I know you know that. Especially reading out loud. Even so, here is your explanation.

"I became a writer because of the feel of the beach. I wanted to write everything down, along with all the stories I've heard from strangers and from friends. And because of Jerusalem, and people I've slept with. A small town in Maine, where we stayed years ago, in an inn with a window on a field of bright blue flowers. And all the words I've heard in my life. Wildflowers, and bobolinks, and the yellow smell of lemons. Telling stories in any way I choose."

Harbinger stood up. He looked a little flustered, even embarrassed. But he put his hands together, to make a soft clapping sound. Then he did it again. And again. And then he walked over to her, and put his warm wool brown suited arms around her, and hugged her. Not the way he would have hugged Carla, but still.

24

whitefish poolesta

Jerusalem Moments moved along too slowly. Arlette joked that she should call her working draft *Jerusalem Seconds*. The characters felt too amorphous. She couldn't see them clearly enough, feel their hands or hear their breathing, though their story seemed a very real part of her life. It was about a Palestinian man named Adnan Aish. Handsome and cultured, very worldly, very thin, Adnan met Annelies Dieter. She was a Communist doctor from Germany. They met at an international reception for a Swedish peace activist, Olaf Heyum. Heyum made peace between Arabs and Jews by setting up a cooperative village in the Negev. The village made money by marketing environmentally helpful products, mops and soaps and lint-free cloths, with "No Animal Products" written on all of them in seven languages.

Annelies was tortured, beautiful, and very articulate. She often spoke of the Holocaust, and of her own ideas about moral responsibility. She was, for her own reasons, enamored of Palestinians. Palestinian men in particular.

When Arlette began writing, Annelies was a Civil Rights lawyer who had once worked for Amnesty International. She was extremely pale.

She gradually became softer, more fleshy. She gained weight, and suddenly wanted a baby. She started to laugh, to become less dogmatic. She stopped her long monologues about her "being Germanness." She started wearing thin bracelets, and laughing out loud when something struck her as funny. Just as abruptly, Arlette changed Annelies's job. She wanted Annelies to be more subtle, less pointed, without having to give speeches on human rights, to Adnan or anyone else. Doctors might talk less. Their infrequent speeches were on smaller subjects: Poison Ivy and How to Avoid It, or what your options were for colitis.

Annelies became a general practitioner. She was interested in alternative medicines, in herbs and acupuncture, homeopathy and massage, in raw foods and macrobiotics. She spoke of healing, rather than curing, and treated many people for free.

She did not work in a refugee camp, or a church-run hospital in Gaza. Instead she went to Jerusalem on a government program, and spent her days in a well-known large and efficient Israeli-run hospital, known for their miracles with hearts. She grew shorter as Arlette kept writing. Not so taut. A little more uncertain of her own path.

Arlette had lived in Jerusalem once. She'd wanted to stay, never pictured leaving. She had been in love with the city, the rich texture of each day, its gold white light, haunting paths of dark green trees on top of old pink stones. Strong smells of those streets stayed with her, sweetish dust, cut onions and lemons, bright fresh parsley and roasting meat, baking pretzels, running children, live camels, new bread. It was a raw, earthy city, cloaked in ancient rituals and hidden sex lives, full of people savage and holy. Compelling Jerusalemites spilling out of alleyways that could barely contain them. Big Arab men on little wooden stools, desert women swathed in long, embroidered Bedouin robes, Israeli men with strong bodies and lime aftershave, modern women, smooth brown beauties, with small pointed breasts, handmade sandals, and very long legs. There are many gods in Jerusalem. Life and death was always present, not in the Leventhal way. Life and death were close together in Jerusalem. She still didn't know, ten years later, why she'd left. When she'd lived there, she taught highschool English. Her students, a little younger than she was, pleaded with her to stay. But she left abruptly the day her program ended. With no real goodbyes.

She kept Jerusalem notebooks, and returned often. Every other year or so, she tried. She tried to write stories, set on the Mount of Olives, or near the Jaffa Gate, in greenish cafés with glasses of gold tea and overly sweet honey cakes. But her stories, for all of their atmosphere, did not hold the smell of those streets, or their heady power either, their sweat and intensity, or their blinding whiteness. She was trying again, with Adnan and Annelies, to piece that life together.

As for Adnan, he was a composite of so many men she'd met the year she'd lived there, serious, high minded, anxious, and naive. Eager lovers with innocent ways. Men she'd meet for coffee all times of day. Men with mothers and wives and countless packs of cigarettes, who held onto her as though they were drowning in icy cold seas. Many men with PhD's. She grabbed back, for the time she was there. But these stories themselves, simple stories of foreigners who meet and who get together for a while, needed something else. Spying, maybe. Or subtlety, or death. Or even war. More sex, maybe. She tried to write hot sex scenes, but they all turned sweaty. Still she felt capable enough to have Adnan and Annelies fall in love.

"Annelies knew, even when they were arguing, that Adnan was a man she'd never forget." Arlette drank water when she wrote, as many glasses as she could. She always used the same glass, a very deep red. The glass made the water look as though it were glowing. She wrote with a number two pencil, thin gray sentences in a clear and tiny script. On the edges of her notes, she wrote many asides, but these were in pen. Nearly relevant details: "I waited my whole life to tell you what I could never put into words."

She wrote names all along the borders of her pages: Electra Silver and Havana Gold, Whitefish Poolesta, Pedro Savannah, T. West. She often wrote names for horses, although there were never horses in her stories: Designated Driver, Berkley Fizz, Sam Odds, Dress Code, Fur Long, El Kayim, Eisek Jacob, Madelyn Mao. She'd always done that, even before she'd ever been to the races. The names formed a Babylonian-sounding poem with a very long middle, and no real beginning or end.

Sometimes, to distract herself from other writing, she wrote whole poems from these names. She wrote them on separate pages, then pasted them together like ransom notes.

> The real true life of *Ana T.*
> *steady Stephane*
> flower *William*
> *deflower Alexander*
> *caring Philip*
> I like you *Daniel R.*

181

I like you a lot Xavier G.
We don't have enough common ground J.
Let's go cross country Amos
Europe Wolf
North Africa Stuart
London Walter
Puerto Rico Pedro
Kansas City, Mo., Robert G.
More than that Albert
inobtrusive, Benign Percy
We should live together Ivan H. / Jaap
We should live apart Serge
I need time Lloyd
I need space Uzi
I need you Ben
I don't understand who you are Alyosha
We will forget what's happened before Jonah
It isn't over.
Don't think it's over.
Ayo

She often thought it might be better, instead of writing words the way she did, to mount them in clear glass frames, hanging them around the apartment like portraits.

Her apartment looked dark all of a sudden, without enough windows. There was nothing she could do.

"Dear Jake," she wrote, on a piece of grainy gray paper, paper that looked like oatmeal. It had that politically correct feel to it. She wished it didn't. "Dear Jake," she wrote a second time.

It's nearly impossible for me to write to you. I waited my whole life to tell you what I could never put into words. It's not that I don't want to tell you the truth. I don't know how. But there is a story that I'd like to tell you. Sometimes I think it's a very simple story, one of those dreams you might have over and over again.

You are standing in a room. It is the most beautiful shade of green you've ever seen, something between Bavarian forest and Grecian sea. Blue moss. I don't know that there's a word for this green, but I know you've seen it. It's silvery, and absolutely unforgettable. You are in this room. It is cool and dense, not like a room at all. More like a jungle those wonderful Brazilian writers describe, elegant and mystical. Full of magical thinking. There are many stories in the room, and within the stories, dreams, hallucinations, and reflections. The room is exotic and unpredictable. There is a kind of violence there, and yet, it is exalted. Dear Jake, I don't know if our relationship is enough. But I also don't know if enough exists. Why are we together? Does this question bother you? Here we are, you and I, two perfectly reasonable human beings. We are as obvious, maybe, as Norman Mailer writing about Madonna. We know too much about what comes next.

Maybe if we change our names. That's not as superficial as it might seem. Ulysses or Hercules might make you a different person. Is that some kind of crazy foolishness? I don't want to be misleading, silly, or insincere. I want to try something else, something new. However small. I have tried this name exercise with Harbinger Singh. He does taxes for a living, as you know. But that's not really who he is. He is the most creative person I have ever met. Bigger than his job, or the task of writing. And also very small. He is petty and ordinary and yet he is very free. That's an unusual combination, I think. He isn't really writing a book. He is visiting me the way someone might visit a regular doctor for health. I've never had this kind of client before. I suppose the rest have been very practical, with goals in mind that they either do or don't meet. His goal is much more amorphous. He seems to want to reinvent himself into a cross between James Brown and Ken Follett. But only for the time he is visiting me. For the rest, he seems obsessed with his ex-wife. I think he still loves her, though he says she is flat and dull, uninspired and predictable, tedious and ordinary. All that may be, but I don't think it matters. My guess is that he loves her, and can't explain this even to himself. He must be very hurt that she's left him. His book exercise is just a plan to win her back.

I would like to know Pali, the sacred language of the Buddhists. It is somehow connected to Sanskrit. I tell you that by way of telling you something new about me, although it is a small detail, not particularly revealing.

"Dear Jake," she continued, drinking a glass of water from her bright red glass.

I am not attempting to be honest. This could all be a technique. Although I consider that idea to be artistically inexcusable. I should begin this letter with the words *Stately and Plump*. Stately and Plump, I've become someone else. A woman who calls you Eizek (instead of Isaac. That e and i seem almost kabbalistic, too unreal.). In a way you are my eyes. So Eizek would be an appropriate name. Although in Hebrew it means something about laughing. But that's OK too.

I wish we laughed more. I wish I were able to call a halt to my own palimpsestic processes, my endless parchmentlike manuscripts used over and over, all partially erased. Can we help each other Jake? Is helping the same as love? If I were to call you Eizek, would we be any different? I still feel a sharp pain in the pit of my stomach when I think about you. Is that pain love?

You have often accused me of ambivalence, as though it were possible not to be. But you know that can't be. There is nothing unambivalent, except maybe the love of a parent for the child. And even that has its own problems.

I've been thinking of buying Harbinger an abacus. I should give him something. I feel he's given more to me. And so have you, my Jake. My Eisek. My semilaughing eyes. I love you, whatever in the world that might mean. At least, today. Your Molly Bloom

P.S. I'm thinking of lightening up on all this white. Ha Ha. It's enough already. I've been surrounded by white for years and I feel ready to look a few colors in the eye. Even changing the whole apartment. Giving it all away, and starting again, only this time, it will all be different. How many times do you think people have said that sentence? A/M/B

Dear Molly, I like Eizek. Didn't you tell me that Harbinger too changed his name? To Tales or Miles or something like that? Or did he change it in a way that makes it fluid? Ever changing, in other words?

Today, I will be Eizek. Today I am a man. Sort of. Whatever a man might be. Saying you love someone seems to have so many implications. I hear this warning sign in my head, something like And Then What? Does it mean we have to have a baby? I know that most of the world is crazy about children. And just plain childhood too. My own was relentlessly miserable. I could not wait until it was over, and I'm not sure I want to inflict that experience on myself again, or on someone else. I did not have good role models. My parents were hopeless, self-involved, and nervous. It could have been worse, I guess. But that was bad enough.

If I did have a son, I'd like to name him after Moses Maimonides, or Ludwig Wittgenstein. Just kidding. I'll bet you think that wasn't a joke. But it was. I don't envision myself playing baseball or soccer with anyone. I didn't play myself. How in the world could I play with him? Girls would not be easier. Besides, you don't pick and choose. You see I am working myself up into a kind of stupor.

If you are not interested in the Jerry Lewis festival at the Forum this week (and you are not the only one, although I wish it were otherwise) I might suggest a different activity for us. Jerry Lewis: another subject we've never gotten to. Whenever I mention him, you start talking about Primo Levi, or something. What a leap. I suppose for today at least I'd like to call you Aretha. Preserving your essence. With a twist. I love you too, of course. (Yes I know there's no of course about love.) Eye.

Two nights later, Jake pressed the buzzer for Arlette. His ring was his own, and she always knew that he was the one at the door. Still she went through the buzzer ritual, out of habit. "Who is it?" she asked into the plastic box on her wall.

"A question for the ages," he replied. "Jason of the Golden Fleece. Odysseus. Moses. Mohammed. Mao. Whoopi Goldberg and Dolores Huerta. Golda Meir."

"OK," she said, "Although I'm not completely prepared for a crowd." But when he arrived at her door, she gladly let him in.

25

his small penis

"You won't believe what I did today," Arlette said to Jake, greeting him with far more enthusiasm than either of them was accustomed to. He moved back a few inches, as though he were reeling. "Come sit down so I can tell you."

"Let me guess," he said. "You edited the word 'consequences' out of a legal book. You told Alice no, when she offered you Rush Limbaugh's favorite recipes. You met one of those people who sent you book proposals. You made peace between Israel and Jordan."

"Guess seriously," she said. "And if you guess correctly, I will give you a large and unexpected surprise. Something you would never imagine I was capable of giving you. Like total acceptance, or black towels in my bathroom. Something on that scale."

"How many guesses seem reasonable?"

"I am confident that even with infinite guesses, you can't. But we don't want to make this too open-ended. Six. But try to think in unpredictable ways."

"You had sex with old Mrs. Israel next door," said Jake.

"That doesn't merit an answer. But no," Arlette replied.

"You took four tabs of acid and are actually speaking Esperanto."

"No again," she said.

"You married Harbinger Singh, as well as his wife."

"Another no."

"You took a job in Billings, Montana, teaching English."

"Another no. Only two more. If I were you, I'd be a little more careful."

Jake sighed, and leaned back into the familiar pinkish couch. "I think you should make a move in the direction of comfort," he said.

"Look who's talking. At least in my house you can sit down without feeling you have to change to match the chair."

"Are you buying black towels so I can move in?"

"Jake," she said. "You're getting low on guesses. You have only been vaguely close with several of your speculations. Very vaguely. One more opportunity, and then, it will be a situation where I win and you lose."

"But what is the prize?"

"Does that matter?"

"OK, you've been saving your money furiously, and you've decided to spend it by taking us both to a remote corner of Belize, to see ruins and birds and lie on the beach."

Arlette stood back. She smiled at Jake, and leaned against the wall. "I wrote my first penis poem," she said, smiling. Jake looked a little pale.

"Don't tell me that you of the bizarre cinematic experience, where anything can happen, find this odd in any way."

"Not at all," he said. "But tell me before you begin to read. Is it mine?"

"The title is 'His Small Penis,'" she said. "What do you think?"

"O.K.," he laughed. "Go ahead. I feel better, I must say. But whose is it?"

"Whose doesn't matter. Listen," she said. "I'd like to repeat the title again. For tonality's sake."

"Believe me, I remember."

But she ignored him. Arlette leaned into the wall. She looked much less tense than usual, almost happy. She looked like she was enjoying herself. "I wanted to try poetry concrete here, so the poem could look like what I was describing, but there are too many words to make this small enough," she said. "If I used very small type, maybe I could do it, but then, it would be too hard to read. Here goes," she said.

And then she began to read in a clear, firm voice, a little louder than usual:

His
Small
Penis

Once, I had
a lover
with a
very
small
penis.

Very
small.
Though
he had
a high
IQ.
Good
salary,
money
enough
for
summers
in Deer Isle,
or Wellfleet,
winter
vacations
in Venice,
Paris,
even
Berlin.
He saw
Hedda Gabler
seven times.
Six
were
poor
productions.
He read
Thomas
Bernhard's
novel,
The Loser,
and liked

it a lot
"beautiful
and pessimistic."
He had two ex-wives,
no ex-children.
He liked
to go to dinner.
His penis
was
terribly
small.
This
was a
constant
fact.
A point
of departure.
It often
came up.
He listened
to jazz
and ordered
good Scotch,
no ice.
He had
a certain
amount
of culture.
He read
Turgenev,
Rushdie
and Isaac Babel.
His mother

was living.
His penis
was small.
He liked
to run,
to play bridge
and poker,
liked horse
racing and
Josephine Baker.
He was OK
as a lover.
Somewhere
in the middle.
Competence
is the word
that comes
to mind.
It was hard
to dream
about him.
Even
in the beginning.
His penis
was not
the reason.
But it
got
in his
way.

When she finished, she smiled very broadly, the kind of
smile she hadn't felt in years. Jake looked shocked. He'd actu-

ally grown pale. He didn't speak for a full minute. And then he did.

"How would you feel if I wrote a vagina poem?" he asked. "Would you construe the act itself as antifeminist? Or is a vagina neutral ground? Is 'Her Small Clitoris' OK? Maybe clitorises are not supposed to be big. I don't know. Do you?"

"Seeing as you've never written a poem in your life, to the best of my knowledge, I'd feel glad. As though I inspired you," she said. "Go ahead. Why don't you try. Any vagina poem is fine with me. Even 'Her Wonderful Vagina,' about someone I've never heard of."

"And another thing," he continued, ignoring her. "Who was this? I'm not jealous. You know that. He doesn't sound like a very romantic character, even if I were. But I am actually very curious. It isn't based on me, is it? Not that the details are accurate. But that could be poetic license. I dislike Thomas Bernhard, by the way. I don't think we've ever discussed him."

"It isn't you. Why would it be? Besides, I thought we had this absolutely unalterable policy of never discussing lovers from the past. We agreed in the beginning of our relationship that it was not a good idea. And if I remember correctly, you were the one who was certain. You did not want our past to intrude on our present. You called yourself antihistorical. Could that be? Isn't that what you said?"

"Don't you think it might be helpful just to know who your partner's had sex with?"

"Why?" she asked, in a tone of voice that made her answer seem unalterable. "How would it help? Let's say we both know about every single partner. From eighteen on. So what?"

"Maybe we'll understand one another better just by knowing."

"Unlikely. What will we understand? That we have, each of us, been attracted to other people? That we've each had sex with some of them? Four or nine or twenty? What about the poem? Did you like it? Enough, anyway?"

"It's hard to separate the poem from penises," he said. "And needless to say, I have an immediate reaction to hearing the word *penis*. But yes I liked it. It put you into a different light. But I like the light you're in already."

"Dogs keep barking outside," said Arlette. "They sound like coyotes. I don't know what's happening around here. The summer's making everyone crazy."

"Are you changing the subject? Come here," said Jake. "We can talk about this again a little later. If that's what we decide. Maybe you can write part two. You can do a whole series of penis poems. Can I suggest the title for mine? How about 'His Magnificent Perfectly Shaped Highly Effective Penis'?"

"Let's just see."

26

still working on it

"Why are all chihuahuas named either ChiChi or ChaCha? A third Cha might be better. Don't you think so? Come here ChaChaCha." Harbinger raised his voice an octave. It was on one of their Wednesday nights. "It seems very un-American to have a rodent-looking dog. They are so tiny and underfed they might as well be from Calcutta. American dogs should be big. They all seem like boys. They give them names of first sons, too. Max and Mister and Tinker and Elvis.

"Chihuahuas seem a little silly. Like crazy eccentric relatives. Do you just take them for granted? Their names, I mean? Having grown up here? Although to tell the truth, the words sound a little Brazilian. Are there chihuahuas in Brazil? That's not the kind of information you'd know, is it Carla?

Or is it?" He looked at her questioningly. He wanted her to answer, wanted very much for her to respond to him somehow. He waited for her to suddenly change her mind. To love him all over again. He knew she loved him once.

He was wearing a grayish suit made from material that looked like the skin of a shiny synthetic fish, a smiling sea creature in a Disney tank. He looked taller, and his humming, which he did not usually do in Carla's presence because he feared she'd be annoyed, was strong and entirely clear. Harbinger usually sang on key.

"What in the world are you humming?" she asked. "Are you singing? That is what you're doing, isn't it? The sounds have a strangled quality, as though something odd is caught right in your throat. Though I don't have much of an ear. You could be Pavarotti. I probably wouldn't know. Singing's my best guess. Am I right, Mr. Singh?"

"Do you hear that, Carla? Even you have some percentage of poetry lodged in your soul."

"It's just that song has a very familiar ring. Have I heard it before? Is it part of a medley? What is it, Harbinger?" she said, impatiently. "Tell me."

"Guess," he said. "I think we didn't do enough guessing in our relationship. We didn't even ask what's for dinner because neither one of us ever cooked. But it may be guessing that keeps coupleship alive."

"Coupleship? Harbinger, I've been terribly worried about you lately. You're just not yourself. Where is the familiar man I know?"

"The dull, brown-suited fool you think you married and divorced?" he said, and stood up for emphasis, moving toward her, and putting his head right into her face. "It's *West Side Story*. The score. Maybe even 'Something's Coming'? How's that for theme music? Does it seem appropriate? In fact, there are no scores that would suit us better. I looked through the music store for music about lawyers, and found absolutely nothing. No 'My Attorney's Bernie,' or 'Attorney on a Journey.' That's not bad. You can't possibly say *lawyer* in a song. Even the word is deadly. Although it's not as alarming as *attorney* or *public defender*."

He took a very deep breath, and began to sing, softly, but directly into her ear: "I like to be in Amereeka. OK by me in Amereeka. Everything free in Amereeka. Delicious coffee in Amereeka Yah."

"Coffee?" she said. "I don't remember that. And there isn't any, besides. Although that is changing very dramatically. Did you take liberties? Do you see that as your prerogative?" She smiled at him with something more suggestive than kindness.

"Yes," he said, "But it's only the very beginning. You can't begin to imagine the liberties I will take."

"Oh, but I can," she said. "That is, I would like to."

"Would you really?"

The waitress, a thin, taut, well-pierced woman, who also looked tattooed although it was impossible to see underneath her clothing, appeared at the table. She spoke in a friendly monotone. "I'm your waitress, Linda Casey. Would you like to hear our specials, or should I come back at a more appropriate time."

"Does Bill's have a new policy of introduction?" Harbinger asked. "We usually have Genevieve, but I don't see her tonight."

"She's no longer Wednesdays," she said. "Her acupuncture apprenticeship classes are Wednesday nights. But," and here she paused very briefly, "I can easily give her a message. We are lovers. Womyn with a y. That's how I got this job." She moved forward a little closer to the table, and whispered loudly, "Bill doesn't know the nature of our relationship.

There's really no need. Genevieve just suggested that a good friend fill in. Bill is very straight," she said, then added, "but his restaurant is fine. It's good in fact. He flirts with Genevieve. I've seen it. She's very cute," she said. "The athletic type. She's in the Triathlon. Everyone always thinks lesbians are vegetarian but that just isn't true."

She leaned back, and seemed to switch roles, formal waitress again. "Our specials this evening," she said, her voice suddenly official, like Walter Cronkite telling America their honest choices for dinner, "include prime ribs at fifteen ninety-five, trout generously stuffed with crab and shrimp, veal francesca with a little white wine and butter, and shrimp scampi. And you know we always have many steak choices. Our house pride. I'll be back soon enough," she said, and turned on her heels, disappearing.

"I'd give her performance a B minus," Harbinger said. "Not good, and not bad either. I liked the revelation rendition more than the menu presentation, I must say. And this is a restaurant, so one would assume that the menu should take precedence, at least from the perspective of the owner. Not over all things, of course. If we were choking, that would be another matter. But certainly for the period of time it's being presented."

"Are you having an affair?" asked Carla. She looked him right in the eye.

"You've asked that question more in the last few weeks than you ever did when we were married. And you know," he paused here for dramatic effect, "you and I are no longer married. So my sex life is not in your bailiwick. Domain if you prefer," he said. "Why would you be interested? Just idle curiosity? By the way, I am happy to tell you whatever you'd like to know."

Linda returned. Without much fanfare, she was there. "Have you had time to consider what it is you'd like to eat?" she asked, Walter Cronkite still.

"We have," said Harbinger. "I assume I am still able to speak for you on that."

"We are divorced," Carla smiled at Linda, by way of explanation. "We have one of those complicated relationships."

"I was married once," Linda said, with more than a little sympathy in her voice. Cronkite fell away. "It was a time in my life I'd rather forget, although sometimes it all comes back to me, hour by hour, with unblinking clarity. He was a brute," she said, "A subtle brute. A typical passive aggressive. I'm much happier with Genevieve."

"She's a wonderful waitress," said Carla. "We like her."

"I'm sure," Linda answered. "She can do just about anything. Don't you envy people like that?"

"Boy do I," said Carla.

"Would you mind terribly if I ordered?" Harbinger interjected. And then he began to hum "Getting to know you." Both women pretended they did not hear him.

"She can sing and dance. She knows thousands of things. She can play soccer and tennis. She's a wonderful camper. She paints like an artist. And she's the most organized person I've ever known. I have to pinch myself, sometimes."

"Why is she a waitress?" said Carla. "If you don't mind my asking."

"She never really dealt with the problem of earning a living," said Linda. "Until now. She got money here and there, without much of a plan. She's becoming an acupuncturist, and I'm studying at the Swedish Institute to learn to be a masseuse. But I was a comedian once, although I'm not especially funny. I was part of a group. Four Lesbian Brothers. We had our moment in the sun. But our lead had a sex change operation. Three wasn't as funny."

"Very good luck to both of you," said Harbinger, a little too loudly. "And all the others in your circle. And now, would you mind if I ordered a steak?"

"Are you married to him or not? I didn't understand before." Linda asked Carla.

"Not now, but we were. You'd better answer him," she added. "He doesn't have a great deal of patience."

"Steak steak steak!" Harbinger bellowed. The room appeared to turn toward him.

"I wouldn't mind about the steak," Linda replied. "Although it isn't terribly good for his digestion." This she directed to Carla.

"Give it to him anyway," said Carla, and the two women laughed together.

"If I might interject a word or two here," Harbinger cleared his throat. "This is a restaurant with steak as a specialty. Perhaps it might do Bill better to hire someone more positively disposed to the cuisine he chooses to highlight."

"That may well be. But I need this job, for reasons I feel no need to go into with you." Linda glared. "What do you know about me anyway?" she asked.

"Far too much, except for one crucial detail. I want a steak, and you are in the only position, as the situation is currently constructed, to bring it to me. So we may be in a bind of unalterable egos." They glared at each other.

"You win," she said. "How do you want it?" Now she seemed like a stranger, an anonymous waitress. Someone with a husband and children in a two-bedroom ranch, who ate dinner on a picnic bench made from a kit.

"Rare and soon. I am hungry." He smiled at her, and she smiled back. "And one additional request. Please don't ask if we are still working on it. That phrase is enough to ruin my entire meal."

"I never would, although it's certainly happened here. It's inevitable. By the way, all is forgiven," she said, as she was leaving.

"Me too," yelled Carla. "One of the same. Rare and soon."

Harbinger looked pained as Linda laughed, and waved.

"I think we should have sex tonight," he began. He looked up at the ceiling, which was shot through with acoustical tiles. In the middle of the room there hung a big brass chandelier in the shape of a lasso, with twelve small cowboy hat shades. "Born on a mountaintop in Tennessee," Harbinger began, pointing at the light. His voice was low, and his manner a little cocky. He shook his head, as though he were wearing a raccoon hat.

"Why tonight?" said Carla, and he stopped singing.

"Why not tonight? Wednesday is our night. It's all the time we have together. We might as well make use of our time in the most intimate possible way. After the steaks. I'm hungry," he said.

She was silent for a minute or two. She didn't look at him directly.

"What about sex?" he persisted. Then he looked straight into her eyes, and she looked back.

"Divorced couples aren't supposed to have sex. You know that, Harbinger."

"If that isn't the most insane rule. Whose is it anyway? Emily Post's? Because she knows as much about sex as the entire British nation. Can you imagine following Queen

Elizabeth's Sex Tips? I'd sooner follow Richard Nixon's. By the way, I'm thinking of including a cameo by Queen Elizabeth in the book I'm working on. A literary walk-on. I would steal the idea directly from the movies. She would suddenly appear, with that hairdo and a diamond watch and a light blue handbag tightly clutched right next to her body. Inside would be a set of royal nail clippers. Don't you think that would be a nice touch? And twenty lipsticks. All bright pink. The reader would know because it would all spill on the floor. The clasp would be loose.

"And she could say something very much out of character. Maybe that she's actually a man. What do you think? Do you think it might add a little something? It also occurred to me that she could be wearing a silly T-shirt. Like 'World's Best Dad.' Her nipples could show.

"I want a lively plot, something with humor and sex and death. I don't yet know how to get it in. Or even, who'll have sex. And who will die. I've even contemplated a medium-sized war. It could be anywhere. India, Africa, even New York City. Although New York's a little less likely. No nuclear warfare, of course. And there will be a major courtroom scene, a trial really. With a complete and well-developed jury. I've already got some of the juror's names. Yoshika Hamada, a filmmaker who makes films about the bowery, and water towers. Marguerita, a post-modern lawyer, and Kermit Kellog, a CPA. We need one, don't you think? Write what you know, and write what you don't know, seem to be the two schools of thought. Kermit will be an antihero, the hardest to convince. He'll ask for facts. Statistics. And of course, facts are a variable entity, as you know.

"In my book, the ruling class would all end up exiled to a small city in Kansas. Somewhere hot and dry, with only the

Bible read out loud on the radio, in a drone. I'd have to go there first, to make sure the details were accurate."

"Do you have a plot, or a title?" Carla leaned forward, very close to him.

"Aha," he said. "I can only tell you this. I began with *Hot and Dusty,* but don't ask me to give you the reasons."

27

some enchanted evening

By eleven, they were inside Carla's apartment. After the divorce, both Carla and Harbinger had moved. She now lived in the west 70s, in a big pre-war building with a lobby full of shadows, old marble, and charm. Her lobby smelled faintly of lavender and onions. On the wall were pictures impossible to remember, no matter how hard the effort: nature scenes, maybe, or children on bicycles and animals romping. The lobby itself was timeless. The floor, a geometric pattern that looked, from certain angles, like a sundial, was green and white and pinkish marble. Nondescript couches, always empty, faced one another around the room. The walls were a color that was nearly brown, and although the space was windowless and dark, it felt more comforting than gloomy.

They entered as though they were part of a procession, points on a couples continuum. Two people whose destiny was wedded to the lobby. Carla talked and Harbinger listened. They walked across the dimly lit floor. Carla talked about health care reform, and how she saw it not happening. Harbinger nodded, though it was hard to know if he was listening. They looked married.

Before very long, they were inside Carla's apartment. Harbinger had never been there before. Carla hadn't invited him, and he hadn't wanted to appear unbidden. Tonight though, he'd insisted, and she gave in with hardly a fight. Could she possibly still love him?

Carla's place had three rooms: bedroom, living room, kitchen. Harbinger looked around, and found it surprisingly pleasant. Much nicer than his. Soft and full with plenty of places to sit, reading lamps, and even a deep purplish vase of long-stemmed red roses. He wondered if an admirer had sent them. Would Carla ever buy flowers for herself? He didn't think so.

"Some enchanted evening," he began to sing, and picked up Carla, lifting her high in the air.

"What are you doing?" she asked very softly, as though she didn't really want him to answer. He kept singing, with a deep-voiced bravado that was sometimes his wont, and carried her quickly into the bedroom. This was all so very familiar, something that seemed to have happened again and again. But had it ever? As he sang and undressed her, Harbinger looked at Carla's body with the awe that comes from seeing someone you know very well completely and totally naked.

Carla looked into his eyes. Her attorneyness had vanished. She seemed much more peach than navy, full of softness and hope. He imagined her whispering obscenities. She didn't, so he kept singing.

"You will find a stranger across a crowded room," and he sat still as she removed her clothing with a purposeful deliberateness.

"I saw that show, and remember every single song," she said. She was smiling, and dazed. "I'm goin' to wash that man right out of my hair," she began, and worked herself up into a rousing finish, surprising both Harbinger and herself. He smiled at her and stared.

Naked, she lay on top of her white chenille bedspread, waiting for him to undress. She was a graceful glimmer in the pale light that entered her room from outside. She looked thin and moonlike, not at all the kind of person who used the word *arguendo* in a sentence.

Harbinger himself undressed slowly. In his apartment, left on his own, he often fell asleep in his suit. Carla looked at Harbinger with expectation. They were very familiar strangers, who suddenly seemed to realize how happy they could make one another. For a while, anyway.

Harbinger wound down his medley. He did a long fade. Carla whispered, "Over here." He went to her quickly, fitting inside her like a long-missing piece from an intricate puzzle. They found one another in the state of dreamlike pleasure that familiar lovers often know.

Carla and Harbinger, together from the start. Eden before the fall. Carla before she turned into Marla, and Harbinger before he started to sing. Together, they were comfortable, silent. They seemed to need very little. Their life could be happy, if they could end it there.

Dear Haldora,

I would like to describe an emotional circumstance. Does that mean I am interested in becoming another sort of writer? Probably not.

People don't change. They just think they do.
Which reminds me, before I get to the actual point
here. I read an interview on the subway in a
magazine someone had left on the seat, with a
famous shaman who is also a seer. He's from a
country called Burkina Faso (it used to be Upper
Volta). He calls himself Some (from Of All The
Parts). Some says that virtual reality and CD-ROMs
connect you with the big cosmos. (He also says
it's all relative, by the way. He is in the
reality-is-a-figment school. He could be right.) I
thought this might interest you because you said
you were uncertain about the computer. 'Is it Bad
or Good' is how you asked the question. He might
say Very Good (I think). Perhaps you should
consider writing your novel on a computer. This is
just a suggestion.

I spent twenty-four hours with Hot and Dusty's
heroine, for research purposes, as well as good
reasons of my own. I tell you this because I would
like to write about it and, perhaps, change the
character of the antiheroine to one of more
compassion. She doesn't have to be hard-hearted to
accomplish the tasks set in front of her. Also, I
thought I should change her profession to Child
Advocate to make her seem more human. More
sympathetic. I no longer want her to murder. Or be
murdered. But I don't know how all this fits with
the notion of plot. Maybe she should struggle with
the baby question. Then more readers could
identify. Where are the emotions in the large plot
scheme that I envision this novel to be? What does
John Grisham do about emotions? And then, if a
character is killed, for instance (you know I have
always thought of myself as a Large Metaphoric
Mystery Writer, for no real reason, I suppose),
how is it possible to have the reader feel concern
and sympathy, but not so much that she can't
continue reading? Is that a real problem, or not?

I found a quote the other day that I'd stuck in a book someone had given me. The quote is from a letter Nathaniel Hawthorne wrote to his wife. I assume you know him. I'd like to use it as a preface for my book:

> Indeed we are but shadows, we are not endowed with real life, and all that seems most real about us is but the thinnest substance of a dream—till the heart be touched. That touch creates us, then we begin to be—thereby are we beings of reality and inheritors of eternity.

What do you think? Does this mean I am not a real writer?

I can't begin to describe my dinner with Carla. The waitress talked a lot. I sang. She even sang! We ate at Bill's. The waitress doesn't like red meat, though that could be a pose. Bill's is a steak house. Hers seemed to me an inappropriate response. I don't know how to judge any more. Did I ever? Would you know the answer to that? Yours, Babu P.S. I have been thinking of going to Lourdes. At work a born-again Korean secretary from Queens mentioned that her church is chartering a plane. She told me that I might be the only non-Korean. I don't mind that. I am usually the only Sikh. I'd like to go. Imagine a Lourdes scene. People being healed all over the place. And I could deduct it, too. How about this? Maybe M/Carla could go to Lourdes, dip in, and come out another person, in love with our hero. Do you like that idea? Has it ever happened?

28

salaam aleykoom

Arlette and Jake talked on the phone very briefly. It was a warm and humid Thursday morning. Arlette still had no air-conditioner, only an old metal fan that clanked when she plugged it in, so she didn't like to use it.

They made a plan to hear the Japanese country folk singer Toma, a modern day Marxist who worshipped trees, and Ry Cooder, in a free concert in the park. If they were still awake and interested, they planned to go downtown to a midnight performance, the first, of an opera based on Leonardo da Vinci's notebooks. The opera was long. The notebooks themselves were five thousand unbound pages of the Renaissance artist's fantasies. Jake wanted to go. Arlette didn't, but felt she should.

She sat in a big green chair near the window, working on her book. She wrote slowly, slow imperfect sentences. Words. Only words. Between sentences, she wrote a long list of names for horses. She felt her list was Harbinger-inspired. She would give them to him as a present: Pinksportcoat, Lima Bean (son of Jack and Giant), Red Jello, Asthma, Diagnostic, Señor Hat, Older and Wiser, Salaam Aleykoom, Hot Pastrami, Dill Pickles, HomeoPath. She couldn't stop herself from writing names. They seemed to fall out of her pen. Maybe she should write a horse race into Jerusalem. But where could it be? She'd seen horses along the Galilee, even ridden them along the Tiberias ridge, but rapid movements in a circle or on a track of any kind seemed wrong in Jerusalem. And camels, although they look odd, even cartoonish, don't have whimsical names.

Then she worked for a while on a time travel memoir, a book someone had sent her that was written by a Native American tribal chief who lived in Berkeley. He claimed to be able to move around in time, to have spent moments that were actual years in both the past and the future. His tenses were confused. Owls were his ancestors. His children were bourganvillia, and deers. He told stories that went on for pages. He called himself Mamuuu, Servant of Moose. Arlette did not think she was the best person to edit Mamuuu. But Alice had begged for help. Mamuuu was a hot property. They paid as much for him as for Rush Limbaugh. He had the biggest agent in the business. Tom Cruise would play him in the movie. He was already gaining weight for the part. Mamuuu himself was huge. He had a following. Harry Potter crossed with Tolkien but nonfiction, is what Alice said.

Reading Mamuuu made Arlette want to change professions.

Hello. May I speak with Harbinger Singh, please?
Does he know what this is in reference to?
Yes and No.
Would you mind being a little clearer?
I don't believe I can do that.
I see. Well how about your name?
Why of course. I am, and therefore this is, Arlette Rosen.
Well, let me see if Mr. Singh is available just now.

"Arlette? Is that you? Are you calling for tax reasons? Don't be embarrassed. Did you receive an ominous white envelope with the letters IRS emblazoned on the corner? Or was it from the state? The other reason might be to cancel our session. But you don't seem the cancellation type. Do you cancel very often? If I had to guess, I'd say No. Am I right? I don't either. Only in uncontrollable situations. And I don't keep clients waiting. The throngs," he laughed. "Anxiously sitting on the other side of this door, in an outer room bedecked with pleasing enough artifacts of popular culture. Silly diversions. Countless magazines documenting the bizarre sexual habits of Michael Jackson, the plodding affairs of coldly regal Jackie, pregnancies and lip evolutions of Julia Roberts, the ups and downs of Lyle Lovett, J-Lo, Monica Lewinsky. Perhaps we should rename it Hollyweird," he said. "And how, indeed, may I actually help? Don't, for your sake as well as for mine, be shy. Just go ahead and tell me. If it is your taxes, believe me, I've seen worse. Taxes are only money. But you know that."

His voice, on the phone, was deep and assured, as confident as a character he would write. His ill-fitting suit was not in his voice. Neither was his gangliness. He just spoke, from a deeply sure place where taxes were as real as rocks, and his words, though not particularly melodic, had their own comfort.

"I called for two reasons," said Arlette. She sounded breathy, although she was sitting in the very same chair all day. She'd hardly moved. Some days she spent all of her day in one chair. Getting up sometimes, but always returning.

"You've asked me about my taxes before," she said. "They're fine. Perfectly OK. I don't make very much money, so the amount I pay seems huge, but that's not really your problem."

"Oh, but it could be," he said, gallantly. "And why, if you don't mind my asking, don't you make very much? My fee for your services, not that I'm complaining, is quite high. As high, as you well know, as any tax accountant's. Are the rest of your authors Trappist monks?"

"That's not why I called," she said abruptly. "I called for no real reason. I'm sorry to have bothered you," she said very quickly, before he had a chance to say another word. Her heart pounding, she just hung up and sat in her old green chair, staring out for a while. It was easier to write than talk.

"Dear Harbinger, You have affected my work. I can hear you singing, and it's not just theme songs, either. It's even Elvis. I hear him in my sleep. He's you. Last night, I imagined a whole verse of 'Are You Lonesome Tonight?' His voice cut right through me, a powerful buttery animal sound."

Here she paused for a few seconds, and then hummed so softly it just might have been a whisper, far away:

Tell me dear, are you lonesome tonight?

Jake smelled like tobacco if it were spelled tabac. Gently pungent, cured and unyellow. He looked moon handsome, so thin, so black and white he glowed. The night was thick and rich and hazy, a night for salty sex, for endless turnings and repositionings, for midnight truths, long voyages, vodka straight from a bottle. For starts and stops. For musical compositions, and ardent declarations. It was a night for war to end, for Yeats and Mick Jagger and Sojourner Truth, for all great ambitions to be spoken, for James Brown and Ulysses, for mushrooms and ecstasy and inexpressible magic. For birds and hamsters and guinea pigs to be let out of their cages, and for wild and raucous chaos, prayerful, ironic, and deadly serious, to take over the world in secretive and certain ways.

Jake seemed changed, for inexplicable reasons. Music in his body became less classical German piano, more Afro-Cuban drums. Nothing about him leapt right out, but the straight line that he was, his puritanical film-buff side, the part of him that could organize a Jacques Rivette retrospective, seemed to have bent.

At Arlette's front door, Jake actually smiled. His smile was warm and open. She smiled back. They were not accustomed to smiling very much at one another.

"I wrote another poem," she said. "A poem about my life." He nodded. "And I turned down a manuscript today, on ninth-century Iranian glass."

"Who in the world would want to read that?" he asked.

"Experts. They told me it was for the audience that loves Benedictine monks. All those people who have signed up for monastery rooms, who want to be there in case it's the end of the world."

"If they knew the world was ending, would they want to buy a book about glass?" Jake smiled again, and then he reached out and held her right into him, very tightly. He didn't speak. He just held her in a way that was loose and full, all promise and knowing.

Arlette reached for his right hand with her left. She led him to her room. Her room had its own very careful order, dustless unalterable logic of neatly folded underwear, one round Japanese paper lamp placed precisely in the center of a bureau, wooden hangers facing one direction, good soldiers in a quiet hired army.

"Mongoose," she said, and placed him on her bed like a rag doll. He stayed still. "I've never said *mongoose*," she explained. "Although of course I have seen it on the page. You are my Mongoose." Jake looked pleased. She removed his shoes very slowly. He lay as still as a mummy, his arms and legs soft curves along his body. He was expectant, wide open and warm like a perfect night in August. Arlette hovered over him, kissing his ears. The usual background conversation was gone. They were both naked, and silent except for the soft insistent sliding of bodies.

Jake left early. The morning light was gray. It could have been five, or ten, or even early afternoon. It was actually a quarter to seven. Jake left, in a hesitant way. He didn't want to leave her.

Arlette kept sleeping. She slept deeply, dreaming of moments. Strangers smiled at her in her dreams. It was a smooth green summer. Wet hot. She walked through beautiful villages, and spent her nights in open rice fields. People were foreign, yet they weren't unfamiliar. They played music with golden bells and silver bowls. She felt kindness. There were no enemies. No relatives. No wars. Strangers who smiled were not so familiar that they were a problem. The days were pear gold, the nights a soft, shiny black. She slept past eight, very soundly.

29

banana splits

"Arlettelah, so tell me." It was the strong, soft voice of her grandmother, Adella, trilling and warm, an old Jew who'd seen what there was in the world and still persisted. Saturday morning, clear and early. Not yet hot. Even earlier in California, where Adella lived. She had her coffee by five every day.

"It's not Sunday. Have you noticed? Probably not yet. I know you kids like to sleep. Who can blame you. When you have your sleep, you have a lot. That and a good appetite. I lost them both years ago. Don't ask when or why. I can't remember."

Arlette was not quite awake. She sat up in her bed and smiled into the phone. Her grandmother's voice, her insistence, her concern, was one of the sounds she loved best. Those sounds were always so much in the background of her life.

"Nothing's wrong. Don't worry. No one died. No relatives. No friends. Not even a neighbor. Where I live the ambulance is like a doorbell. There are enough dead already. Sometimes I think everyone I know has already died. The Big C. Heart. A stroke. When you reach a certain age, your social life's at funerals. Who gets married any more? Although you'd be surprised. Herbert and Anna met at arts and crafts. They were both decorating bottles with colored string. She's deaf and he's legally blind. Now they hold hands at lunch.

"Most of the time, we sit around and make jokes, and talk about the doctor. Sometimes God. Even at my age. But that's not why I'm calling. God is probably the last thing on your mind."

Arlette was still half asleep. She couldn't imagine what time it was in California. Adella had probably taken her walk, read Dear Abby and Ann Landers, written a long letter to a relative, and baked in case of visitors.

"I'm worried about this O. J. boy, and thought I'd ask you for an explanation. I've been thinking about him for years. Nobody discusses his case any more, but as far as I'm concerned, it isn't over. Why did he do it? I still can't think of one good reason. Unless he's crazy. But he doesn't look crazy. Handsome, yes. Self-important? Maybe. Crazy, no. I can't ask your mother. She'd think I'm the crazy one. She always did. 'Ma, what are you so worried about him for?' she'd say. 'Worry about Iraq if you want to worry about something. Don't waste your worrying on him.'

"You know how she is. She doesn't have much patience for speculation. But that's the fun in life. Maybe she's just reacting to me. Isn't it enough already? She's sixty years old. They say that's what happens. It skips a generation," she continued on, a little breathless. "I told you that already. I can repeat myself. I'm entitled. It's the one benefit of old age."

Arlette stood up, the portable phone in her right hand. She made coffee while she listened.

"She's hard to talk to. My own daughter. Look, it happens. With you I can talk. The woman on the radio says maybe it's because I have less invested. But I don't think so. It's not about blood," she said. "She's defensive. From the very beginning. I'd tell her to eat a strawberry. Who doesn't like them? Now you tell me. And she'd say No. Just No. She was a little girl. What was the matter? She didn't want to listen. That's just how she is. She always knew her own mind. That's good and that's bad. She wanted to marry your father, and I could say nothing. Not a peep. She didn't want my opinion. She made that very clear. Not that I didn't like him. He's a little quiet, but you couldn't ask for better. Am I right? You're the perfect witness.

"He's intelligent. He earns a nice living. He respects her. He's neat and clean. He went to college. He looks nice in a suit. He doesn't drink, or smoke. So what that he isn't very exciting. You can't have everything in this life. Maybe the next one. Meanwhile, you try. Especially in the beginning. You cook, you clean, you raise the children, you have a nice enough life.

"When I was young, there was nothing I didn't want. The moon was not too good for me. And I ended up with Louis. A good man. A kind man. A man who worked hard. I wasn't so young. My time was running out. If I married Solly—and believe me I wanted that, all my heart said yes—I know I probably would have been miserable. That's what they said. So I sent him away. Even today I can feel him in my kishkes. After I recovered from Solly, I wasn't any younger. Twenty-four and they called me old chicken, though I had skin like a baby's *tuchos*. So I married Louis. Sometimes you settle. He was waiting. That's how it happened. Hanging around, attentive. He'd bring the flowers on Friday nights. He was nice to my mother. Today there are a lot of fancy reasons, but if you ask me, people get married because the other person's right in front of you. You need mazel to marry for love.

"Forty-five years. May he rest in peace. It went just like that. In life you have to be lucky," she concluded. "It's all a dream anyway. You'll know when you're forty. You're suddenly aware."

"What is luck?" Arlette began to feel herself wake up. She listened more carefully.

Adella ignored this question. "The first time I kissed him," she said. "Stop me if I already told you. Don't stop me. I changed my mind. The first time I kissed him, I thought to myself, 'I can learn to love him.' And why not? That's the way it was supposed to be. Love shmove. We didn't know about it. Who had time. My heart didn't stop like it does in the movies. I wanted it to, but it didn't. Except for Solly. That was another story.

"Should I have had a different life? Am I talking too much, Arlettelah? I worry about you. You're my favorite. I know you shouldn't say such a thing. They say it's a mistake. You tell me why. What does it hurt for you to know. When would you tell the others? You're not in touch. They're nice kids, all of them. Danken Gut. You're not so young yourself, you know. I worry about your future. You seem to me very much a loner. These days that's the pattern. But I don't know any more what is right and what is wrong. Let me ask you this. Wouldn't it be better to have another body in the bed? I don't say children necessarily. Just a body. Louis was warm. He was

helpful. So what if he wasn't Einstein. Einstein himself probably wasn't Einstein.

"Today you've got your careers, your priorities, your emotional space. Everyone says the world is bigger. If you ask me,
your whole generation seems all alone. How can that be any
good?

"I know about the boyfriend. Mister Jake. I don't care
about his religion. He's a Jew, he's not a Jew. I'm a modern
person. I want you to be happy. That isn't easy. Believe me, I
know. Sometimes busy is enough. Are you busy? I can't tell.
You don't say very much. You used to talk. When you were
younger it was hard to get you to stop. On and on. Just like
your grandmother. What made you clam up all of a sudden?
When you were a child, we had to bribe you to be quiet. A
cookie. A candy. Once your mother gave you a whole Sara
Lee. And now, it's the opposite."

Arlette wasn't sure whether her grandmother wanted an
answer. Or whether she just wanted to ask.

"I don't know," she said, falteringly. "I didn't really stop. I
still talk in my head, I guess, but it's mostly telling stories.
Stories about people, and they mostly take place in living
rooms. But sometimes bedrooms too," she added. "Now that
I am older."

"Tell me a story," her grandmother asked. "One I don't
know already."

"You know them all," said Arlette. "But OK. This is a
story I heard a few days ago. About a woman named Rachel,
an ordinary woman about my age. She was married to a man
named Stu. They lived in Madison, Wisconsin. Do you know
about Madison? It's pretty and livable. *Livable* is the word
that people use about places like Brattleboro, Vermont, and
Austin, Texas. And Seattle, everyone's favorite. It's tolerant

there, lesbians and gays and a good bookstore, and a certain consciousness of the world. Black studies. Injustice. The place of women in history. I think people have a lot of potluck dinners and drink good coffee, eat bread with excellent crust.

"Stu taught Latin American literature. He spoke beautiful Spanish, and lived for a while in Madrid. He was forty-seven. He worked hard. A good father. He and Rachel had two children, a boy and a girl. Isaac and Eve. Rachel worked too. She taught art to at-risk children. At-risk means at risk of living difficult lives. It's really a misnomer."

"So what happened?" said Adella. "So far so good. I'm waiting for the punchline. If nothing happens, it's not a story."

"Isaac died in a freak accident. He was crossing the street the week before his Bar Mitzvah. The family wasn't at all observant, but Stu wanted a Bar Mitzvah, for his mother's sake. One hundred people were coming. Isaac was instantly killed."

"Rachel was so furious at life, at Stu, at what happened—she could hardly speak. Stu kept going. He went to school, he cooked the meals, did the laundry. Rachel quit her job. Her Chinese herbalist suggested she take tai chi at the Women's Center downtown. She started going there all the time. She became better and better at tai chi. Five days a week she went until she became an apprentice instructor. The director there, a thin woman named Jena, gave Rachel private lessons. They fell in love. Rachel left Stu. She took her daughter with her and started another life. The End," Arlette concluded.

"There should be a moral, if it's a story," said Adella. "Although maybe it's not absolutely necessary. On second thought, no. I don't think you need one. In this world you can't predict. Who knows what will happen. That was a good story, Arlettelah. I held my breath. Did he get married again, her husband? And was she happy with her instructor?"

"Yes and yes," she said. "To a woman who teaches history."

"Thank God, there's no one left alone. And what about the child who survived?"

"Half and half."

"Abby calls them Banana Splits," Adella laughed. "What a world. I'm going to hang up. Tell me one more story first. You're talking. I'm happy."

"OK," said Arlette. "My friend Gail moved to upstate New York, to one of those beautiful counties where doctors and farmers and carpenters all live together in very small villages. Gail bought a Victorian house. Next door to her is a woman named Tammi. Tammi's had seven children with seven different men. Gail says that every time she has a boyfriend, she has a baby. And then she brings the babies to the fathers. Now she's pregnant again. Gail says this process is Tammi's whole life."

"What's wrong with the boyfriends? That's what I want to know. Not that I understand her either. And those children. What can happen to them? OK. So now, just tell me about the boyfriend. Yours. We'll worry about Tammi later. Or we won't."

"*Boyfriend* isn't the right word for Jake. But you know what, Grandma, I think I love him. I'm just not sure how I can tell for sure. Is there a way, do you think?"

"Now that's a million-dollar question. If I had the answer, I'd be Abby. Or her sister, at least."

The query letter Arlette opened that day reminded her of Adella. She would have laughed.

Dear Arlette Rosen,

I understand from someone (I am not at liberty to
say who. He says you no longer talk) that you have
a sense of humor, so you are the first person to
see my Alzheimer's Joke Book. I've worked on it
for years.

As you know, laughing is very important,
particularly in life's most difficult moments.
Surely some of those must happen to families and
patients who are in the midst of Alzheimer's. To
help them along, I have compiled the 200 best
Alzheimer's jokes I could find, for the first
volume. If the collection is successful, I could
do Alzheimer's Jokes II. Maybe with line drawings
the second time around. I need help in making the
manuscript look professional, so someone will
actually buy it. I don't expect a lot of money at
first. I'm willing to wait.

A little about my background: I am a psychiatric
social worker, with two Masters degrees. I have
worked with Alzheimer's patients on occasion. I
enjoyed it. Also, four of my relatives are in
various stages.

Here is a joke that is more or less typical. By
typical, I only mean from the point of view of how
funny it is. If you like this, you'll like the
other 199. I heard this joke from my friend
Harriet, whose Aunt Minna has it.

George Bush was upset. He hadn't been the
President for a while, and he craved attention. A
friend suggested he visit an old-age home in
California. A guest appearance. The friend
arranged for the visit. George got there and the
people in the home were thrilled to see him. He
shook hands all around, and listened to their
praises. He felt much better very quickly, and was
about to leave when he noticed an older woman in

the corner, sitting all by herself. He walked over
to her, intending to cheer her up. He smiled at
her kindly, then said, "Do you know who I am?"
"No," she said, looking him in the eye. "But if
you ask at the front desk, they'll tell you."

If you'd like another few samples, I'd be happy to
send them along. I have a whole folder. It's just
a matter of Xeroxing.

I think I need help at getting to the punchline a
little faster. People are impatient. They don't
have the time for lengthy explanations. I
understand that. I'm a busy person myself. And I'm
sure you are too.

I'm enclosing a postcard, with the words *Yes or
No.* Please circle your reply. (If you say yes,
I'll send more jokes.)

Yours,

Roscoe Proctor, MA

P.S. I have sent a sample to Nancy Reagan to
consider writing a foreword.

P.P.S. I have a Strokes Jokes sample, too, if
you're interested.

30

language aerobics

Dear Harbinger, Well I am doing something very unprofessional now. I am writing you out of context. Don't ask me why. I'm sure you're thinking to yourself, why doesn't she write to one of her friends. I'll tell you the reason. It's become harder and harder for me to talk to them honestly. With you it's a different story. You're not really a friend, so that's an advantage. I know you are not offended by that. You don't seem to be the kind of person who wants to be a friend. Am I wrong? I've been wrong before. But I think with me you're not looking for friendship. In your case it's not the usual approval either. (I was an English major in college. And I've been reading forever. Book after book with titles like

Dostoevsky's Banana. Books where characters, distorted and misshapen, dream in Aramaic and seek out truth.)

Authors who generally come to me want to know if they're writing something that matters to someone else. Is it a cliché? Has it been said before? Do they have originality or depth or, even better, both? Are their characters alive? Do they have anything to say? Do they have the elusive yet knowable It? Are they sufficiently agreeable, or disagreeable? Are they angry enough or heroic enough? Will their book sell as many copies as *Dianetics*, the Bible, Dr. Spock, and *Mac for Dummies*? Will it become a classic? Will it stay in print more than a few weeks? Will the people they care about buy it? Will it be memorable, and honest? Will it last forever? Will everyone love them because they wrote it?

You seem different. And so I am writing to tell you very honestly that I don't know if I can help. I'd like to help you, because you are unlike any person I've ever known and that is reason enough. But I'm not sure I can.

I am useful to people who like the idea of careful evaluation, people with editing queries about book proposals, about plot and characterization, about dialogue and voice. About how to write a book in the first place. What a book is, and how to make one.

None of that is you.

I don't want to string you along. I like our sessions. I like your songs, and all of your ideas. Hoof and Mouth are good names for characters. Most people call their characters Stephen or Richard or Ann.

I'm not sure if I can help. I thought I should tell you. I hope it's not because I want myself in the clear. There is no clear. Ar(e)

Haldora Arlette, (AH HA)

It doesn't matter. I don't expect to be on the David Letterman show. I'm not the type. I like the chance, once a week, to think about a book I Might Someday Write. To imagine all my characters standing in a line, high-kicking and singing about Bangladesh to the tune of "Oklahoma." I am happy with our sessions. I have gotten somewhere. It doesn't matter where. I am probably happier than I might be if I went to psychoanalysis. Many of my clients go. I see their massive deductions. It may be worth the experience for that. But considerations of my relatives, their differing inadequacies, and the errors of my parents, not to mention my own large problems, would be far less satisfying. By the way, it has occurred to me that you might want to change your name permanently to Green Blueberg. Colorful, evocative, correct. If I had to pick the perfect name for you, that would be it. Green has the right ring, although I'm sure the outdoors is not your terrain. Greenpeace might be the commonplace association. You think about it, and let me know. As to the other, more pressing question: I want very much to continue. What I am continuing hardly matters. Yours in Peace, Trust, Hope, and Taxes,

Wood Bloch

31

millennial video

Dear Arlette Rosen,

Are you tired of oppression? Would you like to
take back the power you deserve, the power that is
rightfully yours? Are you just about ready to
break away from boring, tedious, competition-
driven writing workshops and stifling, oppressive,
master-student relationships that these workshops
(white male driven) breed? Come live, work, write,
edit, think, and read on a feminist Indian
Reservation and renew your healing spirit. Native
American teachings in wellness. Sweats, body-
cleansing, feathers. Hosted by actual Native
American feminists. No ersatz anything here. For
information, contact Tiger Eye. Remember, rites of
passage mark important thresholds, where we need
clarity and guidance. Write today.

```
Dear Rose,

Forget about your pencils and your pens, and even
your computers. It's time for Video Book, the
home-movie of the new century. Your ideas come
alive, using scenic beauty from American vistas in
the background of your life. Video is your future.
Many people know that. Do you? Our VHS Video for
Authors of Books ($33 includes shipping) shows you
how to add backgrounds to your writing: For
instance, carved Presidential heads of South
Dakota can be in back of you when you read. If you
don't have a video camera, you can borrow one.
Someone you know must have one. Check around. And
get ready by buying our VHS Video for Authors of
Books. Just mail $33. The shipping's on us.
VidBook. Bill E. Borden
```

Dear Arlette,

Well, I followed your advice, and did an exercise that I didn't really want to do. I did this just for the hell of it. A new experience for me. I usually do things for a reason, as you probably know. (Except for my singing, but that's about all.) I always have a plan. I wrote a letter to my mother, long dead. It wasn't an easy thing to do. We didn't talk very much, and she's now been dead for thirteen years. My father died the year before her. The funny thing about my father is that all those years he was around I hardly saw him. He seemed to walk in and out of the door my entire life. Home from work. Back to work. Home from work. Back to work. Like that. If I ever do write a book, I'll plan it out first. Probably on all white index cards. Action, characters, you name it. Although maybe not, after my time with you.

Here it is.

My Dear Mother,

I wish you were alive so that I could ask you about your-self, although the truth is, I probably wouldn't. Things don't change, as much as you'd like them to. I would like to be dif-ferent, but probably never will.

I am very sorry about that, but I wonder if there's a way to change what happens between children and parents. Children are the entire world, especially to themselves. I have never grown up from that.

I have no children of my own. I wonder if that will surprise you. Probably not. I was never very good with children. And Carla (you met once or twice) didn't want them either. Children made her a little uncomfortable. They were messy and noisy and out of control. I wouldn't be honest if I didn't add here that I felt the same way. They are too much, really. So demanding, so relentless. How did you raise us? I really don't know. And you don't seem like the kind of person who had all that much energy. I remember you as thin and tired. Was it us? Was it something else? When your friends and relatives got fat-ter, over the years, you got thinner. You really did fade away. When you told me you had cancer, I wasn't surprised. Something seemed to be eating you away. So much of your life, you worked in a store. At home and then here. I wonder if there was a difference, for you. If being there was easier.

Now, while I am writing to you, it occurs to me how infre-quently you smiled. How little seemed to matter. Could that have been right? Did you love my father? He was not an easy man to love. He was never around, and when he was there, he was always preoccupied. With what, I wonder? How fast time goes, and how little it is possible to understand.

Mother, were you a religious person? Even that I don't know. You were so quiet, so dutiful and so preoccupied. You seem to have had no heroes. And yet, you raised all five of us.

We are living the lives you wanted, I think. Though how would I know?

I married Carla because I thought she could make me happy. I just assumed I could make her happy too. I was wrong on both counts, but writing to you, I realize how little I've probably known of happiness. But I too have my dreams. And I guess that's what happiness is. What about you? What did you want from your life? Did you know? Was duty your answer? I wonder if that's what's happened to me. I am a son to you, and I feel I have done badly at that. I haven't been much as a son. Honorable, maybe, but what does that mean without a very tangible love? Or did that matter to you? In your quiet way, you must have suffered. Or is that just a romantic way of seeing your life? Mother, I wish I loved you better. And I wish you loved me better too. How impossible it all is. And how hard we try. Your son Harbinger.

32

one mother

Harbinger and Arlette met for lunch on a rainy Thursday in August. They sat uncomfortably together, two people straining to make pleasant enough conversation. They were in a restaurant on Second Avenue in the 20s called Excellent Curry in a Terrible Hurry. Arlette liked the name. Harbinger liked the food. They met for lunch at Harbinger's instigation. He wanted to see her outside of her apartment, although he didn't know why. She hesitated, told him she needed a day or two to consider. When she hung up, she wasn't sure what it was she was considering. When she called him back to say yes, he was very formal. Clientlike. Why yes, he'd said, when she agreed. And then he suggested the place.

It wasn't a convenient spot for either of them. The lights were fluorescent, so they both looked a little sick. The waitress, a skinny, very pale woman emblazoned with body rings, smiled at Harbinger in an overly familiar way. She was dressed in black rubber. He didn't seem to mind. "Order up," she said, and he ordered for them both, the luncheon specials.

"Well," said Harbinger Singh, and cleared his throat. "Another well." Then he began to hum "I've Been Working on the Railroad." "Can you name that tune?" he asked.

"Why do you sing?"

"Wrong," he said. "But it's your day. Try again."

"Someone's in the Kitchen with Dinah. Now tell me. I really want to know."

"Close," he said. "Three's a lucky number all around the world. I brought you a toothbrush as a gift. A kind of thanks. It's made of ivory. It's odd for me to give you something ivory. Holy Cow and all. I bought it from a man from Senegal standing in front of my office building. A nice fellow. I don't like to think of what his tax situation might be. Ivory on your teeth seems apt. Everyone's teeth," he added very quickly. "That was not a personal remark. What do you think of *The Wolf at the Door* as a title? Maybe it is too reminiscent of Little Red Riding Hood. Though that could be the whole idea. Now there's a story everyone seems to like. What's wrong with it, do you think? I'm sure you must have some ideas on this subject. Have there been many such wolf transformation stories?"

"I thought you wanted to have lunch to talk about your mother," said Arlette. "Say one for yes, two for no."

Harbinger said "One" so loudly the other diners turned around. He raised his right hand for double emphasis. "That was One," he said to the room of lunchtime diners.

"Some enchanted evening you will find a stranger," Harbinger sang softly, humming a whole verse. He seemed more nervous than usual.

"Is that for me?" asked the waitress. "Or is it a general message?"

"I'm terribly sorry," he replied. "But I would have to honestly reply that it is generally meant. Although you seem perfectly well suited to enchantment. Not mine, perhaps. But certainly someone's."

"Do you have a car?" she asked. It seemed entirely out of the blue. "One car?" she guessed.

"Why no," he replied. "After all, this is New York City, and I am not a weekend kind of person. I don't go to Long Island, the Berkshires, or upstate New York. I don't go to Maine or Vermont either. And if I did," he said, "I would probably use a bus. I hope you have not mistaken me for a Yuppie."

"Not at all," she said. "Though we get quite a few of them in here. They don't usually like it though. Too fast. And the fluorescent lights. What did you mean by One?"

"Mother. I was referring to my mother. It was a writing assignment I did for her." Here he pointed to Arlette, who seemed to be watching the two of them as though she were at the theater. He pointed again. Then she nodded. A small bow.

"Are you a writer?" the waitress asked Harbinger. "I know a good story, if you are. My sister's friend's husband kidnapped his two small daughters. She caught him by wearing disguises. But it took three years."

"That is a good story," he said. "But I have one of my own."

"I'm sure you do," she said, and walked away.

"Well," said Arlette. "Was there something you wanted to say?"

"I was wondering what you thought of what I wrote to my mother." Harbinger gulped, very awkward. "You don't tell me what you think very often."

"What I think doesn't matter a lot," she said. "What matters is that you set out to do something, and then you actually did it. My opinion is something else. I liked your letter. I wish I could write one like that myself. I never have. My mother is alive, and impossible. But maybe that's just a part of her job. I'm sure the way I think about her would change if I had children. I would be more sympathetic. It's a very difficult problem, to be someone's mother, or someone's child."

"If you choose to try this exercise," said Harbinger, "I would be most happy to read it. That is, if you would like a reader. I don't mean to be presumptuous. Not at all."

"Why thank you," she said. "But no. You did a fine job," she said. "I could have told you that on the phone. You didn't have to pay for my lunch to hear me tell you that."

"It was nothing," he said, and very quickly stood. "We will leave dessert for another time soon. Perhaps." he added, putting a generous tip on the table. And then they left.

33

eva and max

Jake sounded subdued. His telephone voice could be very intimate, soft air blown into an ear. Or he could be distant, as though he was in a pay phone in Bucharest. "I want to run a Yuppie Redemption film festival here, and they said no. I'm sick of their small, fragile, intimate Hungarian family sagas. Their moving Czech portraits. Their endless Fassbinder Retrospectives. I'd like to try something new.

"*Fisher King, In Search of America, Regarding Henry.* The one where Diane Keaton gives up a wonderful job to raise her baby in the country and make some kind of politically correct baby food. I can't tell you how many of these there are. It's an unexplored genre: Yuppies lose their way by making too much money. Their souls disappear and so do their greater selves. This is assuming they had them to begin with. And then, through contact with a fatal illness, or a homeless person, or seeing war, feeling love, they change their ways. It's a kind of upbeat wishful thinking that seems so American. It might be an interesting way to look at the valuelessness of society. They said our viewers might be offended. It's too close to home. They want respectable esoterica instead. Tony Richardson retrospectives, Paul Bartel's *Shelf Life*. I hate movies where people eat other people. There are even enough for a festival of them. I've had it," he said. "Maybe it's time for alternatives. I could become an activist or a stockbroker or a disciple of the Dalai Lama. It's the Identity decade anyway. Although I'm not altogether through with this one. I'd like to see the downtown puppets. Particularly the Bosnian piece, where knees, feet, hands, and elbows are characters. The word is it's wonderful. Last year they were sold out."

"I should tell Harbinger, although I doubt he would really be interested. For a while he wanted to name his characters after body parts."

"Come on," said Jake. "You must be kidding. I thought Harbinger was Everyman. I thought his life was taxes."

"Not really," said Arlette. "Everyman. That's a mythic idea to begin with. There isn't any. You know that. You could even argue that Everyman has body parts."

"Yes but their names are Pedro or Joe," he said. "Don't be so literal."

She walked to the kitchen while she talked. It wasn't a real kitchen, actually, but one of those small half-rooms, the greenish color rooms become in New York from years of whitewash instead of paint. She had an old half-stove that was mostly burners, and pictures on the wall of advertisements for beautiful pots. Someday she intended to actually buy pots, to spend whole days cooking stews, baking pies, and rolling and stuffing dough with cheeses and vegetables. Now, though, she mostly ate in restaurants, or while she stood up and walked around her small apartment. She often paced, but slowly. Side to side, instead of up and down. She wasn't sure about living alone. True, it was what she'd once wanted. Not to feel hemmed in. And yet she too often heard the sounds of her own breath. If she were a Buddhist, that might be OK. But not as it was.

"Jake," she said, leaning against the kitchen wall. She tried to look at her apartment as though she'd never been there, but found it impossible. "I want to tell you about my dream last night."

"You used to tell me your dreams all the time," he said.

"This one is a little different," she said. "There was music in this dream. And it wasn't the uncertain hum of popular songs. The usual sentimental, conventional stories. Addictive melodies, like Bonnie Raitt or James Taylor. It was more complex and interesting, and what was odd was that I recognized it as a composition by Leos Janacek. Very grand. I could hear how he sublimated some very great desire into art. It was lyrical and lush, the background of a life richly imagined. And yet, I heard that music behind a dream so different from those sounds. In my dream, I was in Miami. I can't imagine a less lyrical place. It's not lush either. Miami is bright blue instead of green. What grows spreads up, instead of across, and the smells are damp, not wet and fragrant. I was alone, in a very big hotel, a hotel with a huge turquoise pool, and an open lobby you walk through like a stage. I walked across, very straight. Almost a dancer. A man was watching me. His son was next to him, and his son was handsome, in his twenties. One of those people with a perfectly linear face. But the son was not nearly so powerful as his father, who had haunting elbows, made from apple seeds, sesame seeds, and what appeared to be pieces of food for a small domestic bird, like a parakeet or a canary. The seeds were hard and tiny, all different shapes. Bird seed trail mix. His old flannel shirt was an indistinct plaid, and there were holes where the elbows might be. His elbows were pointed directly at me. Even though there should be nothing very disturbing about a bunch of seeds, I was shaken by his arms. I could hardly look at him. Why would seeds be so frightening? But they were. There was no flesh there. Only what looked like small sharp pits. I couldn't bear to look at them, and he didn't seem to mind. He smiled at me in a seductive, paternal way, a way that seemed all too familiar. Who do you think he was?"

"You hardly ever talk about your father," said Jake. "Is there a reason?"

"I don't know quite what to say. Maybe I'm afraid of reducing him to a cliché. Of making him ordinary. That man was not my father. I'm absolutely sure."

"Can you tell me a little about him?"

"He was thwarted," said Arlette. "Although I don't know from what, or how it happened. He was often unhappy. Sometimes he was funny. I loved him, but he was barely there."

"Was he thin?" Jake asked.

"No," said Arlette. "He was very white, and very Jewish. He was pale, and worried, and usually preoccupied. He did not sing, or listen much to music. But he knew how to dance, and to play the violin. He did simple magic tricks, like pulling a ball from an ear, and making money vanish. He didn't say too much. My mother talked. Though she didn't talk a lot either. What about yours?"

"You know about my father. He used to play the piano, but not often. He was happiest at the piano. My mother's father set him up in the insurance business, and that's the end of the story. Mort became someone else. A man who'd once played piano."

"Do you think we'll ever have children talking to friends about us?"

"I don't want a son named Max. That's for sure. Even though it seems the thing to do among our peers. Max and Eva. We are reinventing our own histories in some magazine-like way. Max and Eva at Montessori. I see it now. The play, the book, the movie. I won't ever show that movie, unless someone finally agrees to the Yuppie Redemption festival. There are so many possibilities. It could last for weeks. I don't understand their objections. If it were a Turkish Yuppie festival, they'd say yes. I just know it."

"Jake, are you worried about our lives?"

"Are you kidding? I spend every single day full of insurmountable anxiety. And then I go to work, and sneeze, and meet you, and watch movies, and write a line or two, and collapse. Surrounded by appropriate black."

"Is all that enough?"

"I'm not Mother Teresa, Arlette. To pretend would be insincere. I'm not the passionate advocate type. Not really. I have my opinions. Who doesn't? But movies are my way. You might ask my way for what? And then you can tell me about tangible contributions. I could teach a child to write. I could work in a soup kitchen. I could take homeless children to the zoo. But that's not me, either. We are all of us limited in what we can do. We try," he said. "You must know that. Even when it seems we're not. We're trying."

"I think the man with the arms was an omen."

"Good or bad?"

"I wish it were obvious. I really don't know."

"Do you still see Rhoda the psychic?"

"I call her," said Arlette. "Though I haven't called for months."

But as soon as she hung up the phone, she dialed Rhoda's number. Like Adella, Rhoda always seemed to be sitting very near the phone. Rhoda was easy to picture. She was always dressed in a plunging velvet gown, surrounded by airbrushed self-portraits, all emphasizing her extraordinary cleavage. Rhoda's breasts, peachlike and global, large and mesmerizing, were one of her strongest assets. But she had others.

Rhoda, whose nails were perfect orange claws, whose apartment was a balance of gleaming white formica and floor-to-ceiling mirrors, with bottles of Fantastik in a perfect line against the wall, twenty soldiers of them, always full, had as her clientele presidents of companies, PhDs, chiropractors, priests, and two elected officials. She even had a judge as a regular customer. The first time he'd visited, he told Rhoda that he knew right from wrong, but not what was circling around him. All her people were very devoted. They paid her fees in cash, and brought her flowers. They smelled her high sweet perfume and felt comforted that someone was lighting a candle for them, a candle that spiraled upwards into heavens. Rhoda went to weddings very often. She lit candles for money, dispensed advice in a serious and believable way, and read the *TV Guide* as though it were the Bible.

Rhoda held Arlette's hands, the very first time they met, and told her that, no matter what, It Was All OK. Arlette, who wanted very much to believe this, kept in touch. On the phone, she charged for her time, but most questions were answered for a ten-dollar fee. Ten dollars usually bought a reasonable amount of wisdom.

"Arlette," Rhoda said, ageless and breathy. "I have been thinking of you. You are very much in my thoughts right now.

In fact, all day." Arlette pictured Rhoda filing her unblemished nails.

"How?" Arlette asked meekly.

"I see an older friend of yours. A woman who died not too long ago. She had a lot of spiritual powers herself. She was a significant force, but mysterious. She made a decision to pass along all her powers into you. Not right away though. When you are ready. She wants you to eat apples, and sesame seeds, and maybe pumpkin seeds too. Even pistachio, although they are expensive. And fattening. I'm not sure about the pumpkin. I see seeds there though. And when you're full, she will combine her spirit with yours. She will join you, and you will put your powers to good use. I can't tell how over the phone. I have to see your hands. Are they warm?"

"Yes," said Arlette. "They usually are."

"So many of my clients have thyroid problems," she said. "They should do a special." Rhoda hung up abruptly, as though something higher called. And Arlette felt she almost had her answer.

34

two to tango

It was book doctor time. Arlette had waited for Harbinger, and then he appeared. He too seemed eager.

"Has the thought occurred to you that we should be lovers? Because it certainly has occurred to me." Harbinger spoke to Arlette in a very straightforward way, as though what he was saying was not out of the ordinary. Not at all. As right as taxes. He gulped, then continued.

"In fact, it's occurred to me more than once. Not that you are my type, particularly. You are a little bit dry. Very removed. Although removed is one of my specialties in women, as you know. But maybe if we got drunk, things would be different. At least, they'd seem different temporarily.

"You don't seem all that interested in my areas. Namely taxes, something of the law, popular music of all kinds, as you know, and human nature. Though in this last, it's true, we might have an overlap. I must tell you, because honesty seems appropriate now, that Carla didn't share my interests either. Definitely not popular music. She told me she would personally like to murder Johnny Cash and all his country brothers. And as for Elvis, she couldn't even bear the mention of his name. Surprisingly, Carla liked Paul Simon. But I never did hold him against her. I suggest in this case you choose to trust your heart. Just act. Maybe for once you should try something a little unexpected. Me."

"But what if it's embarrassing or horrible or humiliating? What if it changes our work? Besides, I'm in a relationship."

"With Jake. I liked him. But you seem lukewarm. Though that could be your personality. But there's probably something missing," he said.

"Yes I am always lukewarm. That's who I am."

"Someone lukewarm can't write," he said. "Unless you are an academic, in which case lukewarm is a little too warm, a little too personal, for what is required. They want frigid," he said. "Detached. No self exists, except possibly in the confines of the footnote."

"You are using a semantic seduction," she said. "That seems so out of character."

"Words are largely all there is. Did you expect I would jump on top of you in a way that could be considered abusive? Not at all. I am a tax man. I'll hum a few Beatles bars, if you like. I'm governed by order and logic, and an occasional song. Columns are my life. To an extent, anyway. I am not ruled by raw impulse, although the more we talk, I wish you would just remove your clothes. I am curious about your body. It is always so hidden. You're as covered as a religious disciple of Islam. I suppose the more effective way to proceed would be to walk over to you like this. To put my arm around you, and to lean you back, as though we were doing the tango, or some other Latin-oriented body dance. Not the cha-cha, but others. I don't know how to tango, but that doesn't much matter, does it? Here might be a place for me to sing. Maybe Cole Porter, or an Elvis standard. And then," he said, "I can look into your eyes unflinchingly. James Dean, if he were not a homosexual. Popular culture is far more complex than most people think. I would like to look at you and imagine saying something like 'You will remember the next few minutes forever,' or even 'What is about to happen may change your life.' Although that seems a little too melodramatic. How about this? 'We might have a good time. If not, we won't have lost all that much.'"

"What about Jake? Isn't there such a thing as loyalty?"

"Enough!" said Harbinger, and as he put his arm around Arlette he started to hum "If Ever I Would Leave You." He bent her back, a graceful man in a warm brown wool suit, and began, with surprising grace, to remove both their clothes. Naked first, he undressed her with a sureness that was not sentimental or romantic. He was no different naked than when he was wearing his brown wool suit. Arlette, paler and thinner than in her clothes, became more of a flower. Softer, easier, more open to Harbinger, who hummed songs she didn't know.

35

semi-fin

Dear Babu, Dear Harbinger,

What a hard letter for me to write. I sound like a cliché. And you're going to think it was because the sex was not earth shattering. I've had earth-shattering sex. So what. I don't mean the 'so what' exactly. I'm glad for those occasions. But my life didn't change.

I know you're in love with Carla. Even though she might be dullish. You say she talks too much about health care and human services. Imagine calling something *human services*. As though other services were inhuman.

I think you should ask her back. You can still write a book. There are other possible villains. Probably a book with an IRS villain would do very well. The detective can be loosely based on an Indian CPA. He can solve crimes his clients commit. You don't need my help. Use your songs. Maybe he could be a Popular Culture Detective. I don't know much about that category.

So this letter is goodbye. I'm not saying goodbye because we had sex (believe me, it was good enough) but because I can't really help your writing. I can give you exercises. Tell you to write about a secret. Or hatred, or pride, or indifference. But I don't know if that will help.

Stay away from titles like *Anatomy of Water.* Or *Turgenev's Piano.* That's more or less my only real piece of advice. I've spent this summer meeting with you because I like you. I like watching what you do. And having you visit.

That's no different. We can still have lunch once in a while. And do keep writing. It doesn't ever hurt. (Though forget about David Letterman and TV movies. They don't matter.) Yours, A.

Dear A., You're a nicer person than you seem. It was worth the money. I thought I should say that, because money is the valence I know. I don't mean the sex. Yes I agree it was OK. I mean the time we spent thinking *Hot and Dusty* was real. It might be yet. That depends. I think you're right about Carla. I love her, although it is hardly the perfect relationship. None are. Your Babu

Dear Babu, I want the last word. That's just my way. It's going to be hard to decide what that word should be. On the one hand, I want it to be unexpected, a word like *tomato,* or *Hadjj.* Even *bok choi* might be good, although ending with food is against some rule I read years ago.

I don't want you sitting there thinking what could *bok choi* mean? I just like those words. A friend and I used to go to a

Cuban Chinese restaurant on Broadway. His name was Lou. Lou and I would order a dish that was made of bok choi and celery. He would eat all the bok choi and I would eat all the celery.

On the other hand, I don't want to use one of those insignificant catchalls that seem so prevalent. *Ciao* in particular has always rubbed me wrong. (Whereas *Chow* might be OK. Though not perfect.) I want to tell you that our encounter has meant a lot to me. I'm not sure why. But you've helped me, at least as much as I've helped you. (Don't think this is a refund offer. It isn't.) Your singing will stay with me. Don't ask me why. You're right that I've kept my distance (except for the brief foray which neither of us will ever mention again). Now that it's all over I understand how much I'll miss your being around. Bok Choi

36

thirty-six

A thousand times she'd had the thought that Jake was appropriate. Even the word had the wrong sound, far too calculating, as though life were columns of pluses and minuses that might logically add up. She often tried to think clearly about love, about what it might mean, what it might look like. What shape love takes. What it means to love. When Arlette thought about love, she thought about novels. And she thought, oddly enough, about Harbinger and Carla. He loved her enough to write her a book that would win her back. He loved her enough to sing about taxes and rubber plants. Arlette knew that Jake didn't love her, any more than she loved him.

She started to write to him, but she couldn't write a letter without the word *try*. I try, you try, he she it tries. We are all trying. What good is it to try if it's just not there? She called him at work. He always answered on the first ring, as though he were waiting. Was he waiting for her? She wondered if she lacked courage. If she were a character in someone else's book, what would she do? Jake often said that she was a moving target, waiting to be caught. He said she was not even in her own movie. That was his harshest criticism.

He said hello, but he was distracted. He was often distracted. He said he'd been thinking all day about organizing film festivals by professions. Would audiences come to see how films were shot? Or cut? Or costumed? He could start with the truly greats. Imagine, he said, a Storaro festival, scene after beautifully shot scene.

"I called you," said Arlette.

"So you did."

"What if I actually wanted something?"

"Like what? What could you want?"

"You sound impatient."

"Can't you tell me when I see you tonight?"

"Maybe I just wanted to hear your voice. To say hello."

"Are you sick?"

"Do I have to be sick to want to talk to you?"

"Can't this wait until later?"

"I suppose."

By the time they met in her apartment, at eight o'clock exactly, she was angry, though she didn't know why. She suspected what was missing could never be found.

When Jake walked in, he was gentle. He touched the left side of her face, something he'd never done before, and he led her into the bedroom, saying very little. Theirs was not a fierce connection. Their lovemaking was considerate. She lay down on top of her Indian quilt, and he rested beside her. Her breathing was shallow. So was his. They said nothing. The room was eight-o'clock still, very clear and in focus. He reached across her with his arm. His body followed. He rested very close by. She smelled his Italian toothpaste, his light lime cologne. She smelled him with a familiarity that surprised her. Was this love? She didn't think so, and yet, she was afraid that what she thought might be childish, with no larger basis than heartbeats, than dancing, than novels.

"What's wrong?" asked Jake, though he knew.

And then he undressed her. She did not say no because she wanted him one last time. Once more, before it was finally over.

Early morning, she asked him to leave her. To go home. She was surprised at how sad he was, and yet how he did not argue to stay. As soon as he left, she took out an orange notebook she'd bought years before, and began to write. The beginning was simple:

What Harbinger Singh really wanted was a book. Sometimes, when he was being most honest, he would admit he didn't care very much about the subject.

Dear Presumed Book Expert,

My good friend Doctor Nissim Rejwan, noted scholar of Jews in Baghdad circa 1930, referred me to you. He said you are a person of some breadth. My own knowledge range is considerable. That is, I am a world expert on anger in history, and its many manifestations: in ancient tribes, and in many peoples, including Greeks, Romans, Jews, Christians, Borgias, Bonapartes, Roosevelts, Clintons, and scores of others. I have even studied the angers of the Bush family, past and present.

My popular scholarly thesis, "Mad Is OK and Ancient," well received at an anger conference in Copenhagen (I am anti—anger management, by the way) could easily be turned into a very popular book. Dr. Rejwan suggested you for reasonable tweaking.

It's 65,000 words. Long, I admit, but fascinating altogether. What do you say?

Dr. Sasson Sim

Dear Dr. Sim:

I no longer tweak.

Arlette Rosen